TALES OF
CHINKAPIN CREEK

VOLUME II

JEAN AYER

ISBN: 1470135795
ISBN 13: 9781470135799

Library of Congress Control Number: 2012904543
CreateSpace, North Charleston, SC

Jack Wister, Age 16

Carrie Wister, nee Cody, age 16

TABLE OF CONTENTS

ACKNOWLEDGMENTS

I'd like to thank my son Bob Ayer for improving every inch of these stories, and the same goes for my good friend and fellow West Virginian Kevin Meredith. My wonderfully gifted sister Ann Van Saun and my talented nephew Kyle Van Saun provided amazing insights and suggestions.

I'm also indebted to the following writers, aka "The Group": Myriam Chapman, Judi Culbertson, Teresa Giordano, Adele Glimm, Tom House, Eleanor Hyde, Harriet LaBarre, Elisabeth Jakab, Carol Pepper, Maureen Sladen, and Marcia Slatkin.

For my mother

INTRODUCTION TO "TALES OF CHINKAPIN CREEK, VOLUME II"

When George Washington was fifteen years old, he worked as a surveyor along the South Branch of the Potomac River, in western Virginia. His boss was Lord Fairfax, a Brit who, under British law, owned thousands of acres there. George complained mightily about the locals who congregated to watch him work. "They can't even speak English," he said. The people he complained about were my mother's Swiss-born ancestors, who spoke a language known as Switzer Deutsch. Following the Revolution, Lord Fairfax's land fell to my family, who, having squatted there, was allowed to keep it: many thousands of acres. The later fortunes of General Washington are well known. Lord Fairfax died peacefully in his home, Greenway Court, Virginia, and is buried there.

As in Tales of Chinkapin Creek, Volume I, the following stories take place at a remove from George's day. Family names and place-names have been changed, but all are based on the real life experiences of my mother and grandmother.

Big Day In November

We didn't celebrate Thanksgiving when I was a girl. In the War Between the States, our grandfathers and uncles had fought for the South. When Abraham Lincoln made Thanksgiving a national holiday, we refused to celebrate it. On Thanksgiving Day, we butchered hogs.

On butchering morning, Mama kept us children sequestered. Papa was home. Days before, our hired men had stacked firewood behind the old log smokehouse. Before the ground froze, they'd driven forked stakes into the earth to support stout wooden poles. They'd sharpened strong hickory sticks, which we called "gambrels". Our hired men had dragged sleds to the yard and laid boards across them. They'd fastened barrels to the sleds, ready to be filled with boiling water.

In Papa's mind, as in the minds of most farmers in those days, butchering was the very emblem of plenty. It was his family's plenty; his ability to provide for us.

He wore a brown cardigan, a tweed cap and a thick woolen scarf. My young brothers wore versions of the same costume. They dogged his heels and imitated the brisk way he rubbed his hands together.

A dozen hogs watched these preparations from a special pen set up on one side of the yard. Their small intelligent-looking eyes took in every detail. Our hired man comforted me. "They're too fat to be afraid, Nellie, we've overfed them for weeks. They're just restless because they're in a different pen." I knew Reuben didn't believe what he said. It was clear that the hogs knew something terrible was about to happen to them. I found it hard to look at them.

The night before, Papa had made bullets in front of the sitting room fire. With a pair of tongs, he held a bar of lead to the flames and tipped the molten lead into a greased mold. The results were round as marbles and had a shining silver color. I coveted them. What a pretty necklace they would make!

In the morning, while it was still dark, Mama, edgy and distracted, took us children into the sitting room. She had collected willow and alder-wood sticks for my brothers to whittle. I had collected jar lids and teacups for my little sisters to play house. Snow spat against the black window glass. The fire on the hearth crackled. Mama's knitting needles clicked. I read aloud from a big book called "A Child's Garden of Verses."

As gunshots pierced the morning air, Mama flinched. Her knitting needles clicked furiously, as if to drown out the heartrending squeals of the hogs. I covered my ears. Their helpless shrieks seemed almost human.

When the squealing had ceased, Mama relaxed. She gradually came to herself, then ushered us in to breakfast.

After breakfast, we children were allowed outdoors. It was still dark. The sky glowed crimson behind the smoke-house. Steam billowed from kettles over roaring fires. Silhouettes of our hired men leapt against the smokehouse wall as they rolled the carcasses in water, then jammed the sharpened gambrels through the hogs' hind legs. They suspended the carcasses from stout wooden poles, then scraped their skins. Sparks from the fires flew up into the sky.

Papa himself slit the great carcasses from throat to tail. The reeking innards plopped to his feet. He carved each carcass into shoulders, middlings, tenderloins, backs, tails, hams, hocks, feet and jowls. Zinc tubs brimmed with trimmings. The offals—livers, brains, hearts and sweetbreads—were carried to the garden fence and spread across the palings to be cooked for supper that evening.

The spongy pink "lights," or lungs, my brothers used for baiting rabbit traps. The bladders they rinsed, blew up like balloons and hid until Christmas morning. Then they would whack them with wooden boards, creating explosions as loud as gunshots. On Christmas morning, these bladder explosions echoed from every farm in the valley. This pioneer tradition served to let neighbors know that a family was alive and well. Even into the telephone age, it endured as a festive part of the season.

The wooden tubs and soap barrels, that usually occupied our old wash house, had been put away. In their place were set up Mama's big meat grinder, a lard press, and a sausage mill. Mrs. Pope, an enormously fat woman who worked for our neighbor, was lent to us for the day. She, along with her daughter Florence, held sway there in the wash house.

To me, a small child, Mrs. Pope seemed a mysterious and threatening figure. Appearing out of the icy darkness into the flickering steamy light of our kitchen, she wore a bright red apron over her dress of dark flannel that reached to the tops of her high-buttoned shoes. She never spoke and never smiled. She was accompanied by her husband, Welly, an oddly out-of-place fellow. Small and skinny with crow-black eyes, he came along for the pigs' feet, which were our "thank you" to Mrs. Pope.

Tubs of fat were carried into the wash house. Florence fed lean trimmings with some fat through the grinder. Mrs. Pope washed and peeled the linings from the outer skin of the small intestines. She seasoned the meat with Mama's special recipe. She then cranked it into the freshly cleaned translucent outer skin, or sausage casings.

Around midmorning, my brothers and sisters and I materialized, "as if by magic," Mama said, in the wash house doorway. Without looking at our faces, Mrs. Pope handed around the first samples of cracklings—the bits of crisp skin that remain after the fat has been rendered out. Nothing in my life ever tasted as good as those cracklings: warm from the press, crisp between the teeth, melting on the tongue. We chewed slowly to make them last. The delicious fat streamed down our chins. We watched each other solemnly. Mrs. Pope handed around a second sample, but that was all, because cracklings were too rich for children to eat more.

She divided the rest into small crocks to make crackling cornbread. The great bulk of fat she poured into large tubs to be stored on the wash house loft. It would be used to make lye soap.

Mrs. Pope and Florence, who stuck as close to her mother's skirts as a burr to a dog, slipped out to the big yard where Mr. Welly had his own fire blazing. He had appropriated a tubful of pigs' feet. Brimming full, it stood alongside a small pile of sharpened sticks. Mrs. Pope and Florence each took up a stick, selected pigs' feet from the tub, speared them, squatted down and held them over the fire. They pushed off the charred hooves, then scraped the feet and scalded them in boiling water. They would take the results home at the end of the day.

On butchering day, dinner always consisted of fresh livers with milk gravy, and crackling cornbread. From one November to the next, everyone in our house looked forward to this meal.

Supper was special as well, with fresh sweetbreads or brains. If the tired cooks could manage it, we had another round of crackling cornbread. The people who had helped us—our neighbors and their hired man, and all our own people—crowded around long tables. When Welly Pope had eaten, he wiped his mouth on a napkin, then fished in his shirt pocket for a small dark-blue box wrapped in a soft gray cloth. Ceremoniously he unwrapped his mouth organ, tapped it on his palm, put it to his lips, and played "Carry Me Back to Old Virginny." After that he played anything we asked for: "Oh, Susanna," "Camptown Races," "I Love You Truly," or "Dixie." Without fail, he played "Won't You Come Home, Bill Bailey."

One year, as the Popes were about to go home at the end of the day, Mrs. Pope did an unusual thing: she tilted her head back and stared out under her hat brim at the set of tortoiseshell combs in Mama's beautiful thick dark brown hair. Mama saw this. She took the combs from her hair and handed them to Mrs. Pope, who nodded gravely and never said a word.

A year or so later, the Popes acquired a horse and buggy. On Sundays, they took to driving past our farm to the meetings of a small, new, Northern Methodist church. Every Sunday, as we dressed for our own church services, we'd see them drive by. I remember hearing Papa say, "Welly Pope's doing well. He and Almeda are hard workers."

The summer I was fourteen, in 1909, a typhoid epidemic struck the valley. Many people died; one of these was Mrs. Pope. Her huge body couldn't be taken from the upstairs room where she had succumbed. A window had to be removed to get her out. Soon after this, we heard that Welly and Florence had left Guthrie County.

By 1930, my husband and I, and our two small children, lived on the other side of the state. Every summer I came home to see Mama and Papa. One afternoon Mama and I happened to be sitting in her room, catching up on our news, when we heard an automobile outside. I went to the window, and saw a large brown Ford sedan at the back gate.

A tall woman got out, bent down to the driver's window, spoke briefly, then started toward the house. She wore her blond hair in a thick braid coiled around her head, a very old fashioned style by that date. I wore my own hair shingled, as did most women my age. The cut of her dress, four or five inches longer than mine, seemed old fashioned too. The blond woman peered around with an air of taking her bearings, then headed straight for the kitchen door.

"You don't remember me, do you?" she said to Mama and me, but of course we did.

"Why, Florence Pope!" I said.

Florence's husband was the driver of the automobile. He looked so much like her father, small, dark, and skinny, that for a moment I had the impression he *was* Welly. I imagined he might have a mouth organ hidden in his shirt pocket.

"It used to be so cold walking all the way here from home," Florence said. "Ma and Dad and I near froze to death. And then it would be so warm here! And you-all looked so rich. And the food was always so good!"

We'd stopped butchering by that time. Men from a slaughterhouse arrived in a truck, and hauled the hogs away. When they delivered the meat to us, it was neatly sectioned, ready to be hung in the smokehouse.

"I got to thinking about the good fresh meat we used to get at your house. Remember how good home-butchered meat tastes?" Florence said. "I told Ed as we came along the road there, 'I wonder if they have some now.'"

"We might have," Mama said, and gave me the key to the smoke house.

Florence and Ed stood in the yard as if inhaling again the sharp odors of butchering day. I handed them a piece of shoulder meat.

"Dad would've give a pretty penny to of come back here, but my stepmother is a tremendous big woman and traveling is hard for her. Dad didn't want to leave her." That was the last that Florence said to Mama and me before they drove away.

AMOS WISTER

Mr. Amos Wister never perspired. This seems unlikely, but it was true. Other men, working in our fields, were mopping their faces and fanning themselves with their hats, and their shirts were soaked across the backs and under the arms. Mr. Amos, on the other hand, looked as dry and neat in his pressed hickory cotton shirt as if he'd just walked out of a house where he'd been sitting since morning, with the shades drawn.

One scorching August day, a haze hung over the wheat fields, and sweat bees sought shade under the brim of every hat. When the men came in to dinner, Mama noticed their soaked shirts and streaming faces, and remarked, "I can see who's been working hard today."

She didn't see Mr. Amos's quick sidelong glance from under his shaggy brows. At dinner he was silent, which was unusual. After dinner, Mr. Amos took his hat down off the peg, walked out of the house, through the back gate, and turned toward home.

The men on the porch heard the gate's ploughshare weight clang. "What ails Amos?" someone asked.

Papa came back into the kitchen. "Do you know what's wrong with Amos, Carrie?" Papa asked. "The men say he's gone home without a word.

Ola Smith turned from the wash pan. "I know what it is, Mrs. Wister. When they all come in to dinner, you said you could tell who'd been working hard. You know he don't sweat."

Mama turned to me. "Oh dear. Nellie, run and tell Reuben to saddle Lady May."

Mr. Amos's wife, Miz Fan, was an invalid. When she saw Mama arriving at their home, she was surprised and pleased.

Without sitting down or taking off her hat, Mama said, "Fan, where's Amos?"

"Why, I don't know. He's not at your place?"

"He was. I understand he's here now."

Miz Fan was so unaccustomed to visitors that she couldn't focus her thoughts. "Well, you might look out about the barn." She sounded puzzled.

At the end of a path, overgrown with vermifuge and jimson weed, Mama found Mr. Amos. He sat in a little side doorway of his weathered old barn, his straw hat pulled low over his eyes, staring glumly at his hands. He heard Mama, but he didn't move or look up.

She stood a moment, gazing down at the top of his hat. She said, "Amos, you know I didn't mean anything just now. I never even thought about you. You're as hard a worker as any man Jack and I know. We talk about how lucky we are to have you to help us out. You're one of the best friends we have."

He didn't answer. Mama stood looking down at his pressed, cool shirt and neat denim pants. A dew of perspiration stood out on her own upper lip. She took off her hat, and fanned herself with it. It occurred to her that Miz Fan might worry that her husband was missing. She left Mr. Amos, and hurried to the house to reassure Fan.

Poor Miz Fan's sunken eyes lit up. She laughed.

"Amos never sweated a day in his life. We used to joke, him and me, that he's just like an old dog, only he don't pant."

Mama looked with satisfaction at Fan's flushed face. She was glad that this trouble with Mr. Amos had at least done her some good.

Before the day got too far on, Mr. Amos came back to work. Mama thought again of the good that had come of the misunderstanding: Miz Fan had got some company, and Mr. Amos knew his friendship was appreciated.

MAMA AND THE GYPSIES

Mama never begrudged a handout to any of the men who came to our door in the early 1900s. There'd been a depression: these men had fallen on hard times. They'd lost their jobs. They'd been on the road a long time. They wore rags and shoes held together with string. They asked for food, a place to sleep, and work to do.

Gypsies ,too, appeared at our door. But they asked for money in exchange for services, some of which my mother could not identify or understand. They said they'd tell her fortune, but Mama knew this was impossible: only God could do that.

By the time I had grown up, only a few gypsies stopped by our house. They were always female. If any men came, they stayed out of sight to see what luck the women would have. For all Mama's gentle manner, her calm dark eyes, her small, fine-boned figure and lovely face, she had a hard edge about her. The gypsies understood this. She disapproved of bare feet, idleness, and wandering around the country-side, expecting to receive money from honest citizens. She was against lying, which everyone knew gypsy women did when they claimed to know our futures. She couldn't abide thieving, which they were said to do. When gypsy women came to our door, Mama took their arrival personally, as an affront to her own way of life.

15

In early summer, the first gypsy caravan appeared in our valley. A file of dusty, horse-drawn, canvas-covered wagons crawled slowly past our farm lane, inching its way along like a sluggish, spotted snake in the direction of the poor farm. Every gypsy caravan I ever saw headed there, to a lane which led to the river across the road from the poor farm. At the bottom of this lane they had shade, privacy, firewood, and water for themselves and their horses.

My little brothers saw the caravan pass our lane. They ran down to the gate, then came racing back. All flushed with excitement, they shouted, "Mama, Mama! The gypsies are here!"

"Oh they are, are they?" Mama never bothered to look up or pause in her work.

Within a day or two, the gypsies got themselves settled. They then sent out scouts to find corn and oats for their horses, and to see if any horses were for sale, for they were great horse traders. Since every settled person in our valley believed they were kidnappers of children, Mama kept us close.

A couple of Gypsy women appeared at our house. They dawdled up our lane, swinging their long colorful skirts from side to side in a way no lady that we knew would have done. Mama stopped what she was doing, and made her way to the kitchen door. There the gypsy women–always a pair–stood waiting for her.

Mama said, "If you're looking for work, there's work here for you to do. If you've come to beg, you've come to the wrong house. As for telling our fortunes, no one can do that."

The gypsy women never seemed too surprised at Mama's remarks: they knew her by reputation. They'd only decided to make one more try. Alas, they met with the same old failure.

Not everyone in Chinkapin Creek felt as Mama did. When Mrs. Flood heard that gypsies were in the neighborhood, she too kept her children at home, but when a pair of gypsy women offered to tell her fortune, she let them do it. She often said to Mama, "Oh, come on, Carrie, everyone likes to hear about money and handsome strangers. I do. They're amusing."

One summer the pair of gypsy women who arrived were younger than the fortunetellers we'd seen before. They had bright black eyes and were very pretty. After they told Mrs. Flood's fortune (money, travel, a rich and handsome second husband) she said to them, "Now you be sure to stop at the next house. The lady who lives there don't like fortune tellers but she'll like *you*."

She meant Mama, of course.

"That is a very hard lady," the gypsy women countered.

"Oh, shoot," Mrs. Flood said. "I say she'll like *you*."

I happened to be at Mrs. Flood's when this was said. As the gypsy women were the leaving, Mrs. Flood turned to me and her daughter, Maud. "Nellie, you'll find I'm right, those two will surely get your ma. You two run on and watch, then come back and tell me."

Maud and I arrived in time to see the young gypsy women slouched against the kitchen doorframe, one on either side, peering through the screen door. Maud thought they were trying to figure out which one of the women in our kitchen might be Mama. As for me, I felt a thrill of almost unbearable excitement. What if Mama let one of them tell her fortune? What if Mrs. Flood was right? Maud and I dashed around the house to the door on the opposite side of the kitchen. With a jangle of beads, one of the women was just pushing open the screen door. Once inside, she plunked herself down cross-legged on the kitchen floor.

A young hired girl and our housekeeper, Mrs. Pennybacker, were helping Mama slip the skins off scalded peaches. The fragrance of peach juice filled the air. Its color stained their fingers. We saw the gypsy in her finery, sitting on the floor. Her friend loitered outside the screen door. A sweet outdoorsy fragrance, like wood smoke, had come into the kitchen with the gypsy woman.

"If you'll just stop what you're doing," the floor-sitter said, "I'll tell your fortunes, past and present."

Often, when dealing with a situation, Mama gave an impression that her mind was on something else—yet she could appear intimidating. With no sense of hurry, she rose to her feet, and stood looking down at the sitting gypsy woman.

"You should be ashamed, a grown woman," she said, "to sit there on the floor with your bare feet in front of little girls. And how can you know our futures? Only God knows that."

The woman on the floor glanced out at her companion: what they had heard about Mama was true, then. With a rustle of full long skirts, and a clicking and rattling of beads and bracelets, she scrambled to her feet. "Maybe so, maybe so," she muttered. Taking her time, she rejoined her companion. Without haste, they moved across the porch and out to the gate. There they paused and looked back at our house, our yard, and the row of outbuildings behind. Then, skirts swinging, beads jangling, they set off languidly down the lane.

Our young hired girl Ola whispered excitedly, "When I git done here, I aim to run up to Mrs. Righter's. That's where they'll be headed next. I'll get *my* fortune told!"

Then she said in a surprised tone, "Look at your Mama, Nellie."

I turned and saw that Mama had followed the gypsy women out onto the porch. Moving with their unhurried, easy motions, as if trying them out for herself, she stepped to the edge of the porch. Swinging her skirt from side to side, she crossed the yard to the gate, and gazed intently after them. All this took only moments. Soon enough she was back in the kitchen, peeling peaches. Yet she retained, I thought, an inward-looking expression, as if some part of herself had left with the gypsies.

The next year, the gypsy caravan came through the valley as usual, but nobody stopped at our house. The two pretty young gypsy women, who hadn't looked back in time to see her on the porch, would never know how close they'd come, as Mrs. Flood had hoped, to getting Mama.

MR. BUMPHREY

Nobody at our house used tobacco, and only a few of our visitors did, so the smell of pipe smoke on a summer day almost always meant that Mr. Bumphrey had come to tune Mama's reed organ.

We expected Mr. Bumphrey throughout the summer, but never knew exactly what day he might arrive. He was a big, strong-looking man with a shock of black hair and a red face and neck, like a farm hand. His hands and wrists were red too, the fingers short and thick. One day in June, or perhaps July or even August, when it was fine weather, the stage stopped at our gate, then there he was.

One of us discovered him, sitting in one of the big green rocking chairs on our front porch, his derby hat and his cane on his knees, smoking his pipe. Pipe smoke rose fragrantly around his head. His big red face was turned to the view of the river bottom, as if he could see it.

No matter how silently I came upon him, by the side yard, or down the heavy Brussels carpeting in the front hall, he heard me; and knew who I was, as well. "Miss Nellie," he said, "it's mighty nice to see you again, you're getting to be as pretty as your mama," and he gallantly rose to his feet and put out his hand.

His blind eyes looked at me so confidently and he spoke with such sureness that I believed he really *could* see. When he said I was pretty, had he noticed my freckles?

Mama told us children that Mr. Bumphrey did know what we looked like, from the sound of our footsteps and the feel of our hands. My brothers and I experimented among ourselves with this idea. We took turns squeezing our eyes shut while another of us walked by. We never succeeded in recognizing each other.

Papa always sat Mr. Bumphrey next to himself at the table, and helped him to the various dishes. He'd say, "Your meat's on the right side, Mr. Bumphrey. Potatoes are on the left."

Mr. Bumphrey never said, "I know," though we children, watching from the other end of the table, could tell that he did. He really did know his meat was in one corner, the potatoes on the opposite side, and the beans were in between. Mr. Bumphrey touched his red fingertips to his plate's edge as delicately as a fly raising its front legs to a grain of sugar.

My brothers and I discussed whether Mr. Bumphrey could have eaten without Papa's help. I thought he could. I thought he let Papa serve him because he believed Papa wanted to. He didn't want to disappoint Papa.

Mr. Bumphrey had gone to the School for the Blind in Romney. There he had learned how to make his living by tuning reed organs and pianos. He traveled alone to our house. Nobody ever accompanied him. The stage driver took no more trouble over leaving him off at our gate than he did with any of his other passengers. "Watch for the ditch," he might have said, because there was a good size ditch between the road and the short flight of steps that led to our gate. But he never said this, and Mr. Bumphrey never asked. He just went straight to it, without fumbling, and opened the latch.

The day after Mr. Bumphrey arrived, he rested from his trip. From Romney to our farm was only twenty-five miles, but the stage made many stops, taking the whole day to cover the distance. There were stops to change horses, and stops at every farmhouse to drop off the big grey canvas mail sacks.

After supper, Mr. Bumphrey walked in the yard. He paused here and there to enjoy some special thing; a spray of Mama's pink rambler roses on the garden fence, or a long looping branch of one of the big locust trees with its sweet, white, lemon-scented flowers.

He always talked to us children. He was a bachelor, and like the other bachelors we knew, Mr. Perry Hamrick and our Uncle Bill Adamson, he liked children.

"You must be in the fifth reader by now, Miss Nellie," he said to me. I *was* in the fifth reader.

"You've grown a whole head taller since I saw you last, young feller," he told Dayton. Dayton had indeed grown a head taller.

He remembered everything about us. In telling us what he remembered, he was always right.

The next morning after breakfast, he went straight to the parlor. He set down his black satchel, like a doctor's, on the carpet, next to Mama's reed organ, which had been a gift to her from Grandma Cody when she was a little girl no older than I.

"Now stay out of the parlor, children," Mama told my brothers, and sent them on errands. As her oldest child, I had work to do, but every chance I got, I slipped quietly into the parlor doorway. Mr. Bumphrey pulled the organ away from the wall and separated it into two parts. He set the top part, of highly oiled black walnut, with its beveled looking glass and music stand, to one side. The bottom part, also of black walnut, stood open. He lifted away the ebony and ivory keyboard, and the brass reeds. With a tiny soft duster, like a bunch of delicate pinfeathers, he dusted inside the case. All around on the carpet lay screws, bolts, tiny screwdrivers, tiny wrenches. I held myself still as a mouse, hardly breathing.

"Aren't the reeds interesting, Miss Nellie?" he said.

How had he known I was there? How did he know I was looking at the reeds?

"Miss Nellie, will you hand me that screw?" he said.

What screw? I looked and looked.

"There it is," he said, pointing to a tiny scrap of metal that lay near my toe.

How had he seen it if he was blind?

Two hundred forty-four reeds, fifteen stops. In order to tune each reed, Mr. Bumphrey blew into a pipe, which produced soft, low, high, and even shrill tones. In what seemed no time at all, he had tuned the reeds, had them and the keyboard back in place, and the back of the instrument closed.

"Now we'll see how it sounds," he said, getting to his feet. He pulled out a stop here, pushed in a stop there, and sounded each note until he was satisfied.

"Will you help me with the top, Miss Nellie?" he asked. Together we lifted it up and set it in place.

He put away all the tiny tools, like dolls' tools, I thought. He wrapped his tuning pipe in a cloth and replaced all in the little satchel.

"Do you think your mother would like to hear how it sounds?" I called Mama, who had been resting in her room.

Mama twirled the black-walnut stool to her height, pulled out stops and played, "Put My Little Shoes Away." "That's just right," she said.

I think Mr. Bumphrey was tired. After Mama had gone, he went out on the porch, sat down, and lit his pipe.

Tuning the organ took two or three days. I'm sure the job could have been finished in one, but he liked to visit with us. He enjoyed our porch, "looking at" the fields and Papa's new barn and the river. "It's a wonderful place you have here, Mr. Wister," he told Papa.

Mr. Bumphrey, like everyone else who ever came to our house, enjoyed our food. He told Mama, "You set a fine table, Mrs. Wister." He liked the whippoorwills, who sang in our orchard after supper. In Romney, he told Papa, he listened in the early morning to the milk and ice wagons.

On the morning he was to leave us, he sat on the porch to enjoy what he called a "last look." He placed his grip and his satchel on the porch steps, ready to go. Then, with his derby lying carefully on the chair beside him and his cane across his knees, he lit his pipe and turned his face tranquilly toward the road.

"There it is," he announced, presently. He meant the stage.

Nothing was in sight, not even the smallest puff of dust. He rose to his feet, leaned over the porch railing, and knocked the tobacco out of his pipe, into Mama's petunias. He took up his hat and slipped the pipe into his breast pocket.

By the time he got to the gate, a small puff of dust *was* rising, far up the road, on the other side of Mr. Amos's.

Then the stage was at our front gate, and Mr. Bumphrey strapped his grip on the back with the boxes and packages.

The horses, glad for the rest, stretched their necks and lifted now one foot and then the other, and switched their tails luxuriously.

Mr. Bumphrey climbed up in the seat beside the driver. He turned his face to us. "Goodbye, Miss Nellie," he said. "Goodbye, young fellers," he told my brothers. The stage started into motion. We watched him out of sight. He kept his head turned, and watched *us* out of sight too.

OPAL

Amos Wister was a small sturdy man of about sixty, with a shock of gray hair, heavy dark brows, bright blue eyes and a bad limp. In spite of his limp, he did everything on his small farm with only one hired man, and still had time and energy for any neighbor who needed him. In an emergency he was the first to arrive. Papa said it was a wonderful thing just to know he was not much more than half a mile up the road from us.

Mr. Amos's wife, Fan, had been sick for years. They had no children. Mama used to send my brother and me up the road with jars of calf's foot jelly and bouquets of roses. In winter, we took dishes of meat, thick vegetable soup, or pies. When our locust trees bloomed, we took armloads of their fragrant flowers. We were, I suppose, eight and ten years old.

As soon as Mr. Amos's house came into sight, two rangy light-brown hounds came lunging and snarling up to the gate. We never dared touch the latch. A third light-brown hound scowled balefully from under the portico. Mr. Amos came limping around the house, shouting, "Buck, you dog, settle down! Brute, you too!" Buck and Brute slunk away. The third hound put its nose down on its paws, and shut its eyes.

Half a dozen sheep roamed inside Mr. Amos's yard, along with too many cats to count, and chickens of every color, size, shape and condition. The jimson weed and vermifuge, which grew around his well, smelled like the awful patent worm medicine Mama gave us. We would never have accepted a drink from that well.

Indoors, Miz Fan sat hunched in an old high-backed chair, with a patchwork quilt hugged around her shoulders. Her sparse hair stuck out and her wasted hands curled on her lap, like the claws of a dead bird. Cats crouched behind and under her chair, and sprawled on the window ledge and across the tops of her poor thin feet.

"Thank your ma for me," she said in a listless, almost inaudible voice. We stayed only as long as was polite. When we emerged into the fresh air, there on the portico was Mr. Amos. He looked so grateful for our having come, that we felt ashamed to leave. He pressed into our hands a peck basket of Early Harvest apples, a gift for Mama, who loved them dearly. They were mild and sweet at a time of year when only sour Transparents ripened in *our* orchard. It was a treat to bring them home to her.

"Thank your mama for me," Mr. Amos said. Once again we felt chastened.

Mr. Amos's farm had belonged to Fan's family. When she first became ill, he hired a woman to take care of her. As she grew worse, he hired the woman's cousin as well. The cousin was a short, squat, dark-skinned, ugly person with deformed feet. She had an odd way of speaking. "Opal her," she began, referring to herself, or, if she referred to someone else, "Miss Fan her," or "Mr. Amos him." She had come from up on the ridges, where some Cherokee and Shawnee people lived. I suspect she was one of them. She was about fifty years old.

One morning, after she'd been working for Mr. Amos for about a month, she came limping down the road to our house. "Miz Fan her dead," she announced.

We had grown so used to seeing Fan, hunched over in that smelly overheated room, that it was hard to take in Opal's news. But it was true. In her coffin at the funeral, Fan lay wearing the black silk dress, with a pretty lace collar, that she'd put by to be buried in, and a gold pin no one had ever seen. For once, her thin hair was neatly drawn back. Opal had done all that. She stood beside the coffin as if she were a member of the family. She announced proudly to anyone who came close, "Don't her look more naturaler than her did when her was a-living?"

Mr. Amos was, of course, a great target of our local single ladies. They asked him to dinner and brought him cakes and pies and special dishes. Soon after Miz Fan's death, he came down the road and asked to see Papa.

"Jack," he said, "if your Lester and my Lyd got married they could live in your tenant house. Lester worked for us. Lyd, Mr. Amos's hired girl, still lived at Mr. Amos's.

Papa studied his friend's face. It was clear that Mr. Amos had survived a great strain. Cautiously, Papa said, "You're not letting Opal tell you what to do, are you, Amos? Now that Fan's gone you ought to send her packing, and get yourself a proper housekeeper."

Mr. Amos said, "Opal's a good cook, Jack,"

Papa frowned. "You realize, I hope, that Jacob Lytle fathered her last child?"

Mr. Amos flushed crimson, but he stood his ground. "Opal's a good woman, Jack," he said, "ignorant as she may talk. She's cleaned up my house. She got rid of Fan's cats. She sets a good table." He added, "Her brother Ed's a hard worker." By that time, Opal had replaced Mr. Amos's hired man with her own brother.

"Oh Amos!" Papa burst out, "you don't want to get yourself mixed up with that old thing!"

Mr. Amos's flush darkened. With dignity, he rose from his chair and limped out of the room. Papa heard him stumping down the back stairs, then across the kitchen floor. He heard the screen door open, then slam shut. He heard the weights on the back gate clang as the gate swung shut.

That night, he and Mama talked over what had happened. "I'm afraid there's more between Amos and that woman than there ought to be," he said.

Mama said, "At least she's too old to have more children."

For the first time, Mr. Amos didn't arrive to help us make hay, cut wheat and corn, or thresh. In the meantime, up the road, things moved along swiftly according to a schedule Opal must have had in mind all along. Before anyone thought more about it, she and Mr. Amos were married.

Everyone was invited to the wedding dinner, except Mama and Papa. Our old friend Mrs. Flood reported, "To tell you the truth, Carrie, Opal has cleaned that place up. I counted thirty-seven cats the day Fan died. At the wedding there wasn't a single one. And she has those hounds under control. The yard is as clean as any you'll ever see."

The friendship between our family and Mr. Amos seemed at an end. An empty feeling took its place. A vast blank engulfed us, on that side of the road.

In 1916, after I went away to school, I received a letter from Mama. She wrote, "Yesterday, Nellie, you'll never guess who came to the door! Mr. Amos! As if nothing had ever happened! 'Carrie,' he said, 'I've come to ask you and

Jack to dinner.' I thanked him, of course, and of course your father and I went. And guess what? Opal had cleaned up that yard. She's got the fence repaired and whitewashed. I didn't see any vermifuge. And those dogs—they never even made a sound. She's cut back Miz Fan's yellow rose bush. She's filled a plant box with red geraniums. And as for Opal herself, she had on a black silk dress, if you please, and a muslin apron with a yard of lace."

Opal had set Fan's familiar old table, Mama said, with a starched damask cloth and immaculate silver and china. She served fried chicken with milk gravy, snap beans and potatoes, sliced cucumbers and tomatoes, apple butter, smearcase, and light rolls. She had four kinds of jam, Mama said, and a delicious custard pie, seasoned in a way she couldn't guess.

"Mr. Amos didn't exaggerate when he said Opal could cook," Mama wrote.

In the parlor where Miz Fan and Mr. Amos had stood to be married forty years before, Opal had opened Miz Fan's reed organ and set a bouquet of yellow roses on top of it.

As for Mr. Amos, Mama said *his* expression was clear: 'I didn't make such a bad decision now, did I?'

Mama told my little sisters, "You must say 'Miz Opal' now,"

From that day, Miz Opal and Mr. Amos never failed to help us in any emergency. When my youngest brother was born, she sent Mama jelly and fresh flowers. At butchering times, she and Mr. Amos helped out with that hard work.

Around 1919, Mr. Amos died and left the house to Opal. She and her brother Ed kept the place clean and neat, the grass cut, the fences fixed, and the weatherboards whitewashed. Mama sent my sisters up the road as she had sent Dayton and me in the days of Miz Fan.

One summer, when I came home for a visit, Mama asked me to deliver a dish of cornbread up the road to Opal. I was married by then. I lived with my husband and our two little girls on the other side of the state. I took the girls along.

Opal had a wart on her nose: it made her look like a witch in a fairy tale. She wore a clean lace-trimmed apron over a starched calico dress, and a cashmere shawl that had belonged to Fan. Her hair was white. While my little girls hunted for four-leaf clovers and made daisy chains in the yard, Opal and I sat on the portico. Behind us the small house was silent. Ed too had died.

Opal told me that a young cousin of hers had agreed to come and care for her as she herself had cared for Miz Fan. Opal planned to leave Mr. Amos's house to this cousin in return for looking after her.

The afternoon was warm. When I stood up to go, Opal disappeared into the front hall, and came back carrying a peck basket of Early Harvest apples. "Amos him would want it," she said as she pressed the basket into my arms.

Afterward, Mama wrote that Opal had sent her a sprout of Amos's Early Harvest apple tree. She had also given Mama the secret of her custard pie: besides the usual sugar and nutmeg, there was a pinch of freshly ground white pepper.

Cora Flood

Mr. Edgar Flood used a buggy whip on his sons, severely on Royce but even more savagely on Grover. Everyone felt relieved when Mr. Edgar died. His second wife, Cora, would do a better job of managing the boys, everyone said. She felt responsible for Mr. Edgar's abuse and guilty that she hadn't been able to curb it. Mr. Edgar's first wife, the boys' mother, had been Papa's sister.

We noticed a change in Cora soon after Edgar's death. When she visited us, the frantic pace abated in our broad household. Putting the big smoky kitchen to rights after a large meal, making a turn of apple butter, peeling potatoes and setting them to soak; all these things made her laugh. Undoing her bonnet strings, she smoothed the wings of brown hair that grew back from her high forehead. She moved slowly into the room with the serenity of one who had been through hell, and survived. As she did this, a calm descended over us.

"You're so *busy*," she said, laughing. "Life is short, my friends. Life is short."

Mama was young—-fifteen when Papa married her. Mrs. Flood was Papa's age, in her thirties. When Mrs. Flood spoke, Mama abandoned the peas she was shelling. Our hired girls looked up from their pots. I set aside the crock I'd been about to carry out to the milk house. Mrs. Flood pulled out a chair, took up a paring knife and joined us as we got back to work. When Mama happened not to be in the kitchen, Mrs. Flood went to the sitting room. There she hunted through Mama's workbasket for a needle and, as if in her own house, basted together the pieces of Mama's current project.

One day, Mrs. Flood found me ironing a pillowcase. She took it from my hands and lifted a fresh sad-iron from the back of the range. Giving the pillowcase a single stroke from hem to seam, she finished the job. I never forgot it.

* * *

Mrs. Flood's house had a sunny, south-facing dining room. It contained a quilting frame and an old black walnut table, heaped with clean but worn out cotton clothes to be cut into strips and woven on a into rugs. This was an important job in those days, as rugs of any material didn't last long on farmhouse floors.

In her kitchen, something delicious was always being baked, fried or simmered, be it bread, cake, gingerbread or soup. Her parlor contained a stereopticon with boxes of slides to be viewed. A big, brightly illustrated Bible lying open on a table. A basket lay there, full of things to be mended, and a pair of heavy shears. This parlor was very different from any other I had ever seen. Our parlor was kept tightly closed, as prim and tidy as a church, ready to receive formal visitors. Mrs. Flood's was clearly meant to be enjoyed by her whole family.

Her entire farm, in fact, was different from any other. Its front porch was on the back side, away from the road, while its working parts—barns, woodshed, milking pen, milk house, calf lot, and so on were situated in front of the dwelling. It seemed as if the people who lived there had turned their backs on the world. The fact was that they had built it before the road came through, and the farm's arrangement suited Mrs. Flood.

Mrs. Flood's older stepson, Grover, had a restless manner, as if he wanted to be far away from wherever he was. Mama said he had the eyes of a horse about to bolt. Royce, two years younger, followed Grover's lead. When their stepmother's hired men departed for the village in the evening, Grover and Royce followed. Mrs. Flood heard them stumbling home in the wee hours, knocking over the porch benches and drunkenly shushing each other. At dawn, while the cows bawled to be milked and the horses kicked at their stalls, she sent their little half-brother to wake them up.

One morning she burst into their room. "This is a working farm!" she declared. "Do you hear those cows bawling? Do you hear the horses kicking their stalls? Yesterday, Jupiter split a hoof kicking his stall and the smith charged me four dollars to fix it! I cook your meals. I clean the house you live in. I wash your clothes. I need your help!"

Neither of the boys had ever seen her angry. Royce flung a leg out of his bunk, lost his balance, and crashed to the floor.

"I'm sorry," he mumbled, pushing himself to a sitting position, then making an effort to pull on his boots. He knotted the laces and lurched drunkenly out the door.

Grover held his liquor better than Royce. He had slept in his boots. Levelly he said, "Ma. I'm sorry, I really am." He swept up his hat and followed his brother.

* * *

Mrs. Flood told Papa, "They look up to you, Jack. You're their uncle."

"You realize, Cora," Papa said, "the problem is the Finch boys."

"No," she whispered, "The real trouble is that Edgar whipped them. He whipped Grover the hardest. I don't think he will ever get over it."

Papa, surprised that Mrs. Flood understood this, promised to talk to his nephews.

In Papa's study, Grover stared at the iron safe, county maps, and shelves of books. Papa felt sorry for him. But he felt sorrier for Mrs. Flood, a widow with a living to make, a big farm to run, and younger children to bring up.

"Boys," Papa began, "I know your father whipped you. I know that left some scars. But your stepmother had nothing to do with it."

"She could have stopped him," Grover broke in.

"She tried and got her nose broke," snapped Royce.

"Listen, both of you." Papa said, as he raised a hand. "Your father is dead. You've got to leave the past behind. Your stepmother needs you to help on the farm. You've got to sober up, both of you. What do you think your mother, my own sister, would say if she could see the condition you boys get in sometimes?"

"I'll stop drinking, Uncle Jack." Royce broke in.

Grover, as if waking up, said, "So will I."

Royce took charge of Mrs. Flood's farm. He came to see Papa with questions about land use and crop management. Grover told his stepmother, "Ma, I promised Etta I'd stop drinking. I asked her to marry me."

Etta came from a family of Yankee soldiers whom nobody liked, but Cora, a pragmatist, had her tenant house repaired and furnished for the pair to live in, and contributed to the ceremony. It took place at the old Southern Methodist church and was an "open ceremony", which meant that anyone could attend. Mama allowed me to go with Ola Smith. As we arrived, Etta's sisters had just tied the last bouquets of mountain laurel to the pews, and men and women in their Sunday best were crowding in. The organist, my first grade teacher, pumped up the small reed instrument's bellows and struck the opening chord.

Etta carried a bouquet of pink rambler roses and looked amazingly different from the narrow-chested girl I knew. Grover's hair was carefully slicked. He wore a suit, a starched shirt and a pre-tied bow tie. I searched his face for signs of that love which "passeth all understanding" and "saves the drinker from his sins." I saw it ... or believed I did.

After the ceremony, Ola and I followed a queue of buggies and pedestrians. Maud Flood marched in that queue. She had gained a sister-in law! When we reached the porch of Etta's family's little house, Grover kissed Etta, boys rang cowbells, and the audience laughed and clapped!

* * *

Mrs. Flood's tenant house commanded a broad view of the valley. I thought how happy Etta and Grover must be. Yet only weeks after the ceremony, Grover came to his stepmother. "This place is dead, Ma," he said. "Etta and I are going to leave."

Mrs. Flood persuaded him to wait until Etta's baby was born. A month after his son's birth, he found employment at the Florentine Hotel in Vestal, working in the establishment's stables. Soon after this move, Etta, Grover, and their sickly baby disappeared.

Months passed. Papa, at Mrs. Flood's request, eventually found Etta and her child, living in an unheated room behind the hotel. "Grover's looking for work," she said. "He'll come back for Charlie and me." Charlie was her son, and she was pregnant again. Papa took them back to Chinkapin Creek.

Etta's second child was born dead. Our doctor told Mrs. Flood, "Your daughter-in-law should never have had children. She has consumption. She will have to go to a sanitorium. She's dying."

Papa found Grover, living with a prostitute on a back street in Vestal, and brought him back to Mrs. Flood.

"Don't say a word, Ma," Grover said. "Don't say one word! I can't stand it!"

His eyes were bloodshot. He stank of sweat, unwashed clothing and corn liquor.

After Etta died, Grover stayed on at the farm, helping Royce with the work. One clear fall day when the wind blew from the west, Mrs. Flood found a note on the washstand beside his bed. In his cramped hand he'd written, "Ma I've gone to Baltimore."

Years later, Grover died of cirrhosis. He had been living in a Baltimore rooming house. Papa again stepped in, and brought him home to be buried in our new community graveyard.

Royce and Charlie, Etta's only surviving child, sat with Cora in the graveyard. She had tried to shield Charlie from the squalid details of his family's past, though he had gotten wind of most of it. As the pallbearers made ready to carry Grover to the grave, Charlie said, "Grandma, let me see him. He left when I was a baby. I never really saw him."

The hour was late. Shadows of Cora, Charlie, Royce, and the coffin stretched across the graveyard. Cora unlatched the coffin lid. Charlie looked down at his father. Cirrhosis had taken its toll. Charlie showed no emotion as Cora smoothed the wrinkles in the corpse's trousers.

When Cora died, Royce continued to work the farm he had so successfully managed. Charlie graduated from a prestigious medical school in Baltimore, and became a doctor who specialized in the treatment of alcoholism.

OLD SANTA COMES EARLY

In December, we children couldn't help but notice one of our biggest turkeys being carried out to the chopping block behind the woodshed. Afterward, it hung, dressed, to freeze in the smokehouse, to be sent to our Uncle Hugh in Philadelphia for his Christmas dinner. We couldn't help but notice how unusually busy Mama's hands were. The mending, which occupied her the rest of the year, had been put away. We hadn't seen her bone knitting needles in a year. Suddenly, there they were in her quick little hands, producing scarves, hoods, socks, gloves and mittens.

After supper one evening, embroidery needles, floss, and embroidery hoops appeared in Mama's room. Soon, she and I were embroidering doilies and hemstitching hand-kerchiefs and towels, to give as presents. Mama faintly traced monograms on handkerchief linen. Using simple stitches, we filled in the pattern. We crocheted and tatted lace borders on tea towels, hand towels and pillowslips. My brothers rolled old socks into balls, which Mama stitched through and through until their shapes were taut and hard. She helped them cover the balls with leather, and presto... baseballs!

I was the oldest child in our family. One wintry morning, Papa and I drove off in the buggy for Minerva, our county seat. "Christmas is coming," he told me, "I need your help."

As we rolled along, he said, "How old are you now, Nellie?"

"Twelve," I said.

"What do you think about old Santa?"

He watched my face carefully. I studied his. What did he mean? In a moment that I can only say dazzled me, it dawned on me what he was driving at. "You're Old Santa!" I cried, "You and Mama!"

How pleased I was to be let in on the secret! I felt grown up, responsible, practically an adult. I sat silent and amazed, all the way to Minerva.

In the little town, Papa and I bought Brazil nuts and almonds, stick candy, horehound lozenges, and small toys. Tops, Barlow knives, dolls, and games, Santa would fit them all into my sisters' and brothers' caps on Christmas morning. We bought warm gloves for the inmates at the poor farm. Papa was Overseer of the Poor, so this was his responsibility. We bought a supply of small brown paper sacks and plain boxes to sort our candies into.

Bumping over the rutted winding road, we drove home in the winter darkness. My heart was full to bursting. I was so proud of my new status.

By the light of a buggy lantern, Papa unhitched Bashaw. It was late. The children were asleep. We carried the bundle, wrapped in the extra blanket we used on winter drives, into the quiet house and straight up to the big unused bedroom over the parlor. Mrs. Pennybacker had left supper hot for us on the back of the kitchen range. We forgot that the next day was Saturday, and that on winter Saturdays my little brothers and Bess often played hide and seek, ranging into rooms that were closed off and unheated.

The next morning, Mama and I sat sewing by the fire, watching a light snow fall outside the window. We became aware of an unusual silence in the house. Mama put aside her sewing, and I did the same. The silence went on. Then came a clatter overhead, then a spate of excited whispering, followed by a great scampering down the stairs. The sitting room door burst open, and three wide-eyed children wedged into the doorway, "Mama! Nellie! Come see! Come see what we found!"

Papa and I had forgotten about leaving Old Santa's bundle in the cold front bedroom.

Mama reacted calmly. She studied the three little faces. "What did you find?"

"A bundle!"

"Oh, a great big bundle!"

Mama turned to me. " What do you think, Nellie? Do you suppose Old Santa could have brought something ahead of time? Do you think he'd have wanted to lighten his load, so he wouldn't have so much to carry on Christmas Eve? Why don't you run up and see."

She kept the three small children at her knee. I flew up the stairway and down the hall. There, on the big bed in the cold room, was the bundle Papa and I had left the night before. I backed out of the room and shut the door.

Back downstairs, I told Mama "I do believe that's just what happened. Old Santa must have brought something ahead of time."

"Well," Mama said calmly, "Whatever we do, we mustn't go in there again. I'm sure Old Santa's unhappy to know his things have been found. What if he comes back and takes it all away, and then doesn't come at all for Christmas?"

Dayton's brown eyes grew even larger. Hugh's little face was pale. Even I felt uneasy: what a terrible thought, that Old Santa might not come back at all!

At last, Dayton edged reluctantly out of the room, followed by Hugh and Bess. As the door closed, I heard him say, "That's just the old blanket Papa uses in the buggy. That's just a lot of things Papa and Nellie got in Minerva. There ain't any Santa Claus." I opened the door.

"Of course there's a Santa Claus, Dayton," I said. "There's a Santa Claus and you know it. You ought to be ashamed of yourself for saying such things."

Hugh turned on Dayton accusingly. So did Bess.

Later, I went up and moved the bundle to the attic, where no one ever went without Mama's permission.

Then I went down the hall to Papa's room, got a pair of his boots, carried them to the big front bedroom, and slipped them over my shoes. A dusting of new snow had blown down the chimney and across the broad sandstone hearth. I walked into the chimney place and out again, leaving the prints of the big boots, as if someone large had come down the chimney and gone back again. I shut the door, returned Papa's boots, and crept downstairs to tell Mama what I had done.

The next morning, before we dressed for church, Mama suggested we all go into the big front bedroom and check on the bundle we'd seen there the day before. "If it's still there we'll know Old Santa hasn't come back and that he isn't upset that we found his things. Let's hope that's so."

Dayton seemed less sure of himself than he had the day before. We children fell into step behind Mama. The three little ones' faces looked serious. We filed up the stairs and down the hall to the closed door of the big front bedroom.

It was Dayton, the disbeliever, who wrenched the door open. He stared, then cried, "It's gone! Hugh! Bess! It's gone!"

"Oh, looky! Looky!" he shouted, pointing to the evidence on the hearth. "There's Old Santa's tracks!"

Mama said, "Old Santa has come and taken away his bundle."

I looked at my brothers' and sister's faces. They stared back. It was one thing to hear Mama say it, and another to see it. The horrible question was plain. Would Old Santa come back?

Dayton was the most worried of the three. He had been the one to suggest that there was no Santa Claus. There was a good chance that Old Santa was mad at him.

Mama gave us a compassionate look. "I believe he'll come back – if you're good."

Her gaze lingered on Dayton's clever brown eyes. He was a lot like her, full of energy and ideas. "You'll have to be very, very good. You have to be very, very careful until Christmas comes."

The rest of that day, the house was unusually quiet. Mama and I noticed how often sudden silences came over the children, in the midst of their play. They exchanged looks, staring gravely at each other, then turned away. Only two days remained before the great day itself.

At long last, in the early light of Christmas morning, we all trooped into Mama's and Papa's room. Dayton was the first to see the caps just visible in the growing light from the window. They bore their same load of treasure as in Christmases past.

"He did come!" Dayton shouted." He did come! He did come!"

"He did!" Bess echoed.

Hugh, in his relief, burst into tears.

"You see," Mama said, "You've been good, and Old Santa has forgiven you."

I was relieved. Just before we entered Mama and Papa's room that Christmas morning, I, too, had a flicker of doubt that Old Santa would return.

OLA SMITH

O ne day in 1906, Papa stood by our farmhouse gate
with a man named Jim Smith. "This is my daughter
Nellie," Papa said. "She's eleven. She's a big help to her
mother."

I blushed. I *was* a big help to my mother, and proud to
be told so.

"I have a girl a little older than her," Mr. Smith told
Papa. "She's a big help to *her* mother too. If you need her, let
me know." I felt a twinge of rivalry. I hoped Papa wouldn't
hire Mr. Smith's daughter.

Mr. Smith was the man who brought us paw paws,
hickory nuts, skinned gray squirrels, homemade maple
sugar, chestnuts, chinkapins, and persimmons, which he
carried across North Mountain. In return, we gave him
home-cured hams.

That evening, Papa said, "Carrie, Jim Smith says he has
a girl old enough to work for us.

Mama looked pleased. "We can certainly use the help,
Jack," she said.

My heart sank.

Papa asked me to go along when he went to hire and
bring back our new helper. I didn't want to go, but felt I
needed to size up my rival.

Papa drove our horse Bashaw to the schoolhouse, where
we turned left and entered a steep secondary road, which

followed a narrow creek-bed past a few small farms. Around noon, we came to an unpainted post office. Papa handed Bashaw's reins to me, then disappeared into a grove of cedars. After a time he came back, accompanied by Jim Smith's daughter. She didn't look old enough to leave home. As Papa handed her into the buggy's rear seat, I felt her pale eyes focused intently on my back, taking in every detail of my hair and clothing.

Whenever Papa traveled, he pointed out the sights to his passengers. Before a big old house, grown over in Johnson grass and cedars, he said, "That's the old Hunter place, Nellie." Before an overhanging rock, he said, "There's a spring under that ledge, girls. I always pick cress there for Nellie's mama."

To everything Papa said, Ola kept silent. All the way home, I felt her eyes on me. When we arrived, our housekeeper told me, "Nellie, show Ola where to put her things. Then both of you come back here to the kitchen."

In our housekeeper's room at the top of the back stairs, Ola stopped in her tracks to stare into a bit of mirror nailed above the dresser. In a measured tone she told me, "I have lots of pretty clothes at my house. Boys are a-dying to marry me. My pa says I have to help you folks out so here I am. But I won't stay if I don't want to." After this peroration, she turned squarely around and transfixed me with her unnerving stare.

In the kitchen we found Mama, who said in her sweet soft voice, "Ola, we want you to feel at home here. We want you to feel you're part of our family."

"That sure would make one big old family if you-all lived with *us*," Ola said. "There's fourteen of us kids at home."

Ola didn't say another word, but gaped around our big kitchen. She sized up the polished nickel-trimmed range, the red-dyed pine cupboards, the oilcloth covered table with its long well-worn benches, and the sheepskin covered rocker by the window.

I was jealous of Mama's tone with Ola. That was how she talked to *me*.

Soon after her arrival, Ola and I sat peeling potatoes in the kitchen, when a knife clattered to the floor. Ola leapt to her feet. "Pick that up!" she shrieked. *"Pick it up! Quick!"*

I intended to pick it up–of course. But what was the rush? If she cared so much, why didn't *she* pick it up?

"Quick!" she screeched. *"Quick! Quick!"*

Somewhat cowed, I picked it up.

"Now wipe it off!""

I obeyed this, too. As if there'd been no crisis, she sat down again and reached for her pan of potatoes. Her pale, short-lashed eyes met mine. "If your drop a knife and don't pick it up, a man will come a-visiting," she said. "If you drop a fork, a woman will come. A spoon would mean a little child."

She went on. If I stepped over a child who was lying on the ground, and didn't step back, that child would stop growing. If I sang before supper, I'd cry before morning. If my right eye itched, I'd see somebody I hadn't expected to see. If I rubbed my eye, somebody would make me cry. If my left eye quivered on Christmas day, someone close to me would be gone in two months. The first man who came to our house in the New Year would bring good luck. If a woman came, *look out!* If the woman was a widow, I was to take her by the hand, lead her quickly out through the front door, then in again through the back door. If I dropped a horse's hair into water, it would turn into a snake. If I dropped a dishrag, company would come no matter what I might do to prevent it, so I might just as well put my house in order. If I washed my face with a dishrag, I would grow a moustache.

One day Ola and I were putting away the breakfast dishes, when my friend Maud Flood came by. Ola said, "I bet you can't find any freckles on me."

Maud had a faint dusting of freckles, something like nutmeg on a custard pie. Mine were big as the speckles on a turkey egg. Freckles were so unfashionable that ladies avoided them by wearing deep-brimmed sun bonnets, and carrying parasols.

"I used to have freckles just like yours," Ola announced, "but I washed my face in the dew on wheat, and they went away." She narrowed her eyes at us. "You have to do it before sun-up and it has to be the first day of May, and if anybody sees you the spell won't work."

A calendar hung above the sink. May first was the next day. "You have to do it tomorrow," Ola said. "Otherwise you have to wait a whole year."

At that season, Mama had all of us children helping with spring cleaning. Mrs. Pennybacker and I pushed feather ticks out the upstairs windows. My brothers, in the yard below, dragged them to the clotheslines where Ola and a helper beat them with cane rug-beaters. As the feather ticks hit the ground, I imagined my freckles vanishing.

The next morning before dawn, I crept down our dim dew-drenched lawn to the road, climbed over the rail fences, and dropped into the field of young wheat. With cupped hands, I gathered dew from the prickly stalks, then rubbed my face, throat and arms.

Down the road, Maud did the same.

In the kitchen, Ola shrugged sleepily into her apron. She took a long wooden match from the match safe, scraped it against the safe's emery strip, and touched the flame to the paper twists in the stove. The scents of phosphorus and burning pitch-pine filled the air. I handed her the small shovel we used to empty ashes from the big stove's firebox.

She turned and stared at me. "You done it?" she asked.

"I did."

"Maud too?"

"Maud too."

On the lower porch, a small looking-glass hung above the comb case where our hired men cleaned up when they came in from the fields. I stared at my reflection.

"I still have freckles!" I told Ola.

In her irritating, know-it-all voice, Ola said, "Was it the dew on wheat?"

"You *know* it was."

"Did anybody see you?"

"Of course not."

"*Somebody* saw you. Some old tramp was a-laying in that wheat. *He* saw you."

It was hard to give up hope. It was possible that a tramp had seen me. Tramps came through our valley often in those days, looking for work. Though tomorrow was May second, I decided to try again.

The next morning, I checked the wheat field for tramps. I looked in all directions for anybody who might witness my presence. Seeing no one, I quickly cupped my hands into the wheat, harvested as much dew as I could and washed my face with it. For good measure I repeated the ritual then returned to the house.

The kitchen door flew open. There stood Mama.

"Nellie Wister, what were you doing just now in the wheat?"

"You saw me? Aaaaw! Now it won't work."

"What won't work?"

Sighing, I confessed: "Ola said if I washed my face in the dew on wheat before sunup, my freckles would disappear."

Mama gave me a reassuring smile. "Nellie, your freckles are pretty. Nothing you can do will make them go away."

I felt a searing flash of anger at Ola. Had she done this to make me look foolish?

"Ola is superstitious." Mama went on. "We are not. She hasn't had the advantages you have, Nellie."

The tone I had missed had returned to Mama's voice. That tone belonged to me. "People who haven't had your advantages can believe these things," she said, soothingly.

Out the window I saw Ola headed down the yard toward the mailbox. Noticing something on the ground, she froze, then bent over to examine it closely. With an abrupt urgency, she hopped over the item, then back again, turned around twice, then ground it into the grass with her heel. How small she looked then, how vulnerable and uninformed. As she proceeded on to the mailbox, I realized that my rivalry with her was over.

MR. LEVI EADS

Every May, a strange sight appeared in our farm lane: a haystack-like bundle of brooms, broomcorn, hickory withes, white-oak splints, and hickory saplings moved slowly toward our stile. As it approached, we could barely see a horse's legs under their load. When it came to a halt, a small man dismounted. Mr. Levi Eads wore the broad-brimmed black hat of a pacifist sect known as the Dunkards. He lived in the neighboring state of Maryland.

Mr. Eads hitched his gentle, old mare to the stile. Very slowly, the slowest I ever heard any man speak——he said, "Well...children...and...how...are...you-all...this...time?" He turned to his horse and searched in the bulging saddle pockets for a tiny scrub broom and two wooden whistles.

He said, "This...is...to sweep...your...playhouse," as he presented me with the broom.

"These...are...to call...your...dog," he told my brothers, as he handed them the whistles. Mama appeared and, as always, greeted him with special warmth.

He moved with the slowest, most deliberate steps I ever saw, yet he stood firm and upright, for he was an old soldier. He was hardly taller than I, at seven years old.

Mama saved things for him to fix: there were splint-bottom chairs that needed their joints tightened, a table that wanted steadying, corner brushes and mauls to have their handles replaced, and a new basket or two. Mr. Levi's baskets never wore out, but they occasionally met with accidents. His baskets were the only kind I ever knew—stout, double-lobed, woven of hickory withes. There were bushel and peck sizes, and the lovely small egg basket, which my sisters and I loved dearly. I've heard them called "buttocks baskets," but we would never have used such a term, nor felt comfortable with it. Mr. Levi's baskets grew polished with use, and never cracked or split. Their handles came to feel as smooth as satin. Besides scrub brooms, Mr. Eads made regular brooms from the broomcorn which we grew for him. He took the leftovers away to replenish the supply he'd brought with him, and to make brooms for our neighbors.

The first thing Mr. Eads did was go out to the wash house, take down a big zinc tub, fill it with water, and set his hickory withes to soak to make them pliable. He then spent a day or two resting from his long ride from Maryland. Wearing his flat-brimmed black hat and the black shirt and pants of a Dunkard, he sat very straight-backed and soldier-like on our shady front porch. He sat on the child's chair I sat on, when Grandma Wister braided my pigtails, with his small feet planted flat on the floor, hands on his knees. His alert brown eyes gazed curiously at our black walnut trees, our fields and orchards, and the river beyond. As a child, near his size, I felt he was not an adult but almost a contemporary.

If it rained, he sat in the sitting room. There he looked around, examining each object: the wooden mantel clock, Mama's medicine cabinet beside it, the big press in the corner, the long oak table with its collection of newspapers and magazines. He took in the double bed and trundle bed tucked under it, Mama's sewing machine and workbox, the curtains she and Grandma had made of bleached and starched feed sacks, as well as the open door to the hall.

Without his hat, his halo of frizzy white hair, brushed back from his high, domed forehead, made him look like Santa Claus who, in my day, wasn't the fat old fellow he is now. I felt that Mr. Eads saw through me and knew my every thought.

Papa gave Mr. Levi the honor of returning thanks at the table. In the evening, he invited him to lead us in prayer. Mr. Levi never prayed long. That was one of his many charms.

Mama once said, apropos of nothing I can remember, "After what Mr. Eads has been through..." and hurried on with her work. What did she mean? I wondered. What had he been through?

After his days of rest, Mr. Eads moved out to the wash-house. He sat in its open doorway, in the warm sunshine that streamed over the threshold. He laid the dripping hickory withes across his leather-aproned knees, and wove them into new chair seats and baskets. I watched his small hands twist and fold them in well-practiced, graceful motions.

"Mr. Eads," I said, "Mama says you've been through a lot."

He stopped working, and looked at me.

"She's talking about the war," he said, and resumed threading in a withe and binding it tightly. "I was fourteen," he said. "They burnt our Dunkard church. It didn't have a steeple. They didn't know it was a church."

"Who was 'they'?" I asked.

"You've heard about Antietam?"

"Yes," I answered.

The sun beat down. He didn't take his eyes from his work. "Our meetinghouse was on the Hagerstown Pike, close to Antietam Creek. Yankees blew it up, every board and rafter. They razed Moomaw's house. It was on high ground overlooking the battlefield."

"But Dunkards don't fight," I said.

"They destroyed our homes. They destroyed our meetinghouse. They burned our wheat and killed our cows and horses. After the battle, there we were in the middle of empty ravaged fields, homeless. Not one member of our congregation lifted a hand to protect us. They thanked God that things weren't worse. I was outraged! 'Worse?!' I shouted. 'Thousands killed! Everything we own destroyed!' 'We're *safe*,' they said. I felt sick. I ran away. I joined Imboden's Brigade. May God have mercy on me for the lives I've taken."

"I'm sorry, child," he said next, "I forget sometimes who I'm talking to."

At Gettysburg, a memorial lists the men who fought in that engagement. Private Levi Eads of Company One, Sixty-Second Regiment, Virginia Infantry, Imboden's Brigade of Irregulars, is among them. On another battlefield—New Market—Imboden's Brigade is remembered for fighting alongside the cadets of the Virginia Military Academy who, ages sixteen to eighteen, lost a fourth of their number.

I don't think Mr. Eads fought for the North or the South, or even for Maryland. I believe he fought for the Dunkards who, in his opinion, hadn't the guts to fight for themselves.

Grandma and Grandpa Cody and grandchild

AUNT LILY

Aunt Lily was Mama's sister and closest friend. She looked up to Mama, and Mama felt protective of her. So Lily's sudden and unexpected death devastated Mama. The year was 1901. Mama was twenty-four. Aunt Lily was eighteen.

Aunt Lily and their young brother, John Henry, were walking in a field with Grandpa Cody's driving dog, "Collie." Lily carried a basket of blackberries she and John Henry had been picking. They saw a cow that had just given birth. Aunt Lily told John Henry to run and, "Tell Pa that Pet's had her calf."

As John Henry ran to Grandpa, there came a mighty *clap* of thunder: Aunt Lily and "Collie" fell to the ground.

Grandpa Cody, capping wheat shocks a mile away, heard the clap, and hurried toward the sound. Two miles away, Mama heard it. It woke my baby brother, who began to cry. Papa rushed into our house. "Oh Jack," Mama cried when he reached her, "Something terrible has happened!"

When Grandpa Cody got to Aunt Lily, he found her lying flat on her back, with blackberries scattered around her. "Collie" lay beside her, stretched out the way a dog will on a hot day. Aunt Lily's skin was bright pink. Her boots stood upright beside her, empty, their buttons blown off.

"She's going to be all right!" Grandpa Cody cried, seeing her bright color. "She's only stunned! She's going to be all right!"

She was not all right. The women who laid her out found a black burn mark five inches long at the base of her throat. She was still that bright, hot, rosy color.

Aunt Lily's room, usually messy, was neat that day, as if she had tidied it for a trip. The parlor, too, was neat, where the evening before, Willard Morgan had called on her and given her a wide, gold ring. On the music stand of the old reed organ where she'd had played for him, the hymnbook lay open to two titles facing each other on opposite pages, "'Tis the Harvest Time," and "Remember Me."

Aunt Lily's death threw Mama off balance. Her family was staunch Presbyterian, but at the funeral, as the minister strained to find some meaning or purpose in the tragedy, Mama shook her head negatively, almost imperceptibly.

Papa did his best to console her, but he never ventured into religious discussions. He was a Methodist. Mama disapproved of Methodists in general, and this difference between them had nearly prevented their marriage.

In the days that followed, Mama often rode down to the field where Aunt Lily had fallen. She sat there in the saddle, staring at the spot. The scattered blackberries had germinated and formed a circular patch in the middle of the open field. Mama stared and stared at the green sprouts pushing up.

She sat so long, so silently, staring with such intensity, that I wonder if at those times she questioned her faith. She lost weight.

The Northern Methodists had no church in our community, and no regular preacher. The summer Aunt Lily died, they erected a tent and hired a very good-looking young man they called an "evangelist." He wore a black long-tailed coat and a black string tie. Mama's friends found excuses to go hear this handsome stranger preach. It was August, two weeks after Aunt Lily's death.

"Come and hear Mr. Sheets preach at the tent meeting, Carrie," Miss Annie Cudlip coaxed.

"Oh no," Mama replied, "Those Methodists shout and carry on. No, thanks."

"That's just the evening service," Miss Cudlip persisted, "the morning service is quiet. It'll take your mind off Lily. It'll be a comfort."

Comfort was what Mama needed, so the next morning she appeared, wearing a beautiful tan handkerchief-linen dress, carrying her best hat. Over her dress she wore a riding skirt. "I'll be back for dinner, Sally," she had told our hired girl.

At dinner, she looked preoccupied. After dinner, Papa watched her with concern as she disappeared into her room.

Mama attended the Northern Methodist meetings four days in a row. On the fifth day she appeared in our kitchen wearing her old calico wrapper. She sat down in front of a pan of apples and began to peel them. Our hired man announced that Lady May was saddled. "Thank you, Reuben," Mama said, "I'm not going to any more tent meetings."

The next morning I answered a knock at the door. There stood a tall, very good-looking man dressed in a black long-tailed coat and a string tie. With him was a stocky man I recognized as Mr. Dickerson, a local affiliate of the Northern Methodists. Wiping her hands on her apron, Mama joined me.

The man in the tailcoat said, "Mrs. Wister, we feel there's something in our service that troubles you. We've come to ask what that trouble is."

Mama surveyed him the way a skilled marksman surveys a target.

"There *is* something," she said, and led the way to the parlor. She waved her guests to two upholstered armchairs. She herself sat on a straight chair.

Don't say I didn't warn you, Dickerson's expression conveyed to his colleague.

"If I understand you," Mama began, "you believe in 'witnessing.' By 'witnessing' I understand you mean confessing one's sins in public. According to you, if I'm to get into heaven, I must 'witness.' Now you must know, Mr. Sheets, that two weeks ago, my sister was killed by lightning. She was a member in good standing of our Presbyterian Church. She recited the Westminster Shorter Catechism and was awarded a copy of the New Testament, covered in olive wood. She played the organ at Sunday services. She never heard of you or your 'witnessing.' She never confessed to any 'sins.' She never gave in to any 'experiences.' Now, because she never did any of those things, do you mean to tell me she hasn't gone to heaven?"

Mama had won prizes in school for debating.

Mr. Dickerson pushed back his chair. "I'm afraid Mr. Sheets and I have made a mistake in coming here," he said.

"Indeed you have," Mama agreed, getting to her feet.

From the front door she watched her callers climb aboard their buggy. I believe she'd hoped that they'd have said "Oh, no, Mrs. Wister. The Lord makes special dispensations for such exigencies." But they hadn't. She closed the door quietly, stood for a moment in thought, then went back to work.

* * *

That October, Mama traveled to Martinsburg to stay with Papa's brother and his wife. Their church, alas, was Methodist. Mama took a short walk and discovered a Presbyterian church not far away.

One of Uncle Pent's fellow-parishioners challenged her, "Mrs. Wister, we were disappointed not to see you at services yesterday."

Mama gave him the penetrating inspection she had given Mr. Sheets and Mr. Dickerson in the parlor at home. "Mr. Newcomb," she said, "you don't really think God wants us to make such a fuss about worshipping Him, do you? He isn't deaf, you know."

"You Presbyterians are too cold, Mrs. Wister," Mr. Newcomb flashed back. "You might as well be Quakers."

One evening Mama told Papa, "Jack, some preachers say Lily's in Hell, others say she's not. And they're all trying to convince me there's some 'purpose' in her death. They say it's all part of 'God's plan,' but I just can't see it."

Papa put his arms around her. "Carrie, Lily is *not* in Hell. And as to why it happened, the 'purpose', there isn't any." Mama turned to me. "Nellie, go up to bed."

"Stay where you are Nellie," said Papa, "You're old enough to hear this. Carrie, bad things happen. They just do. Preachers say there's a 'purpose'. They're only trying to comfort you. The ground around these hills is full of iron pyrite. It's an ore that attracts lightning. Poor Lily was just unlucky. It's not a comforting explanation, but where is it written that there will always be a comforting explanation?"

Mama murmured, "That's the first thing anybody's said to me that sounds right. Why didn't you say this sooner, Jack?"

"I kept quiet till you asked me." Said Papa. "I'm Methodist. Remember? You might not have liked what I had to say."

"No," said Mama. "I like it."

Dusk turned to dark. Lightning bugs filled the yard. Like so many human lives, they burned brightly for a time, then winked out. Mama and Papa went bed, and so did I. I believe Mama slept soundly that night.

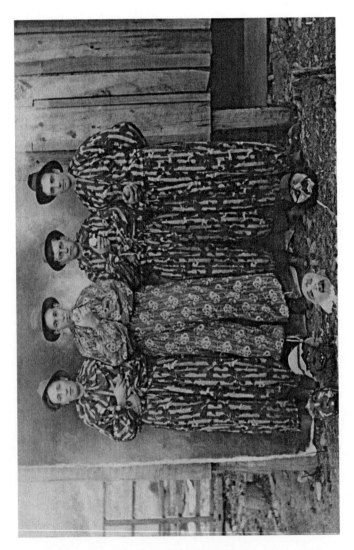

Belsnicklers, Chinkapin Creek West Virginia, Circa 1905
Courtesy of The West Virginia State Archives

WE TURN AWAY BELSNICKLERS

The word "belsnickle" comes from the German, meaning "St. Nicholas in fur". Since many citizens of the United States are of German descent, the holiday tradition of belsnickling was popular when I was a girl. During the nights before Christmas, men and boys put on various disguises. They darkened their faces with soot or stove blacking, pasted on false moustaches, pinned poke-bonnets together to hide their noses, and donned bed sheets or other exotic costumes. Standing well out of the lamplight that streamed from farmhouse windows, they called out in falsetto voices, "Will you let the belsnicklers in?"

I pressed close to Mama's knees. I whispered, "Mama, the belsnicklers are here." Firelight cast scary shadows across the room, but I took comfort in the fact that Papa was home.

Mama laid aside the copy of "Pilgrim's Progress" she'd been reading to us. She moved down the hall and opened the door to a rush of icy winter air.

The belsnicklers carried banjos, tin whistles, Jews' harps and fiddles. They performed skits and sang "Polly Wolly Doodle." "We're poor unfortunate men," they crooned. "Won't you give us something to eat?" One of the singers was given a smack on the rump by his companions, then they all lined up and we had to guess who they were.

My brother Dayton had a knack for figuring out their identities. "That's one's *Reuben*!" he shrieked, "those are his trousers." Reuben uncovered his face and winked at us all.

After we guessed who all our visitors were, Mama offered them cider, sugar cookies, and sometimes, apples, shelled butternuts, hickory nuts or black walnuts. Because our visitors had other farmhouses to call on, they bowed exaggeratedly and bid us good night. The next day at school, someone would knowingly ask, "Did you-all have any belsnicklers last night?"

One Saturday, Mama and I sat in the sitting room making Christmas presents for the younger children. They had gone to bed, as had our young hired girl, Ola Smith. Papa was away at his office in Martinsburg. Because December can be a slack time on farms, our hired men had gone home to their families. Our tenant had finished his evening chores and retired to his own house. A fire crackled on the hearth. The room was lighted by a flickering coal-oil lamp.

"Will you let the belsnicklers in?" came the traditional call.

Why, I thought, would belsnicklers appear when the men were clearly absent? Wasn't it too early for them, more than a week before Christmas?

Mama set aside her needlework and crept out into the dark hallway. I followed. From a window, we made out three shadowy figures standing just short of the window-light.

I felt a presence behind me. Ola. Then Dayton.

"Sssh!" I told them, "Somebody's outside".

"I was afraid of this," Ola whispered, "I dropped a knife this morning."

The familiar call came again: "Will you let the belsnicklers in?" We made out two figures under our old plum tree. One was dressed as a tramp; the other as a clown; the third was harder to discern. He stood apart and kept his face averted. He carried a guitar.

"Mama, do we know anyone who plays a guitar?" I asked.

She shook her head.

The three figures moved close together, as if to consult. They appeared to be appraising our house.

Mama, Ola and I crept through the dark hallways, checking doors and windows. The night was still. When we looked out again, the strangers had disappeared. Were they coming around from behind the house?

"Bullfrogs!" Ola whispered.

"Hush, dear," Mama reproved her.

"Bullfrogs are starting to croak," Ola persisted, "If those men were still here, the bullfrogs'd be quiet. Crickets too!"

I didn't sleep well that night, and I doubt Mama did. Ola put her nightcap on backward and announced that we could be sure this would protect us all.

Whenever Papa was away, Mr. Fred Tolley checked up on us. He came the next morning before breakfast.

"Did you have belsnicklers last night?" he asked.

"Somebody came," Mama said. "We didn't let them in."

His face turned white. "You know my Molly helps old Mr. Honecker? This morning she found him on the floor. He said, 'I thought they were our own belsnicklers!' They stole three big candlesticks and took a ring that had been his wife's. While Jack's away, you better keep some of your hired men here at the house.

The next day, news came that old Mr. Honecker had died.

* * *

In the new year, Mrs. Flood gave a party. Some of her relatives attended from across the mountain. During the festivities, my brother Dayton suddenly stood up and pointed at Mrs. Flood's cousin. "You're the one with the guitar!" he said. "You're one of the belsnicklers we wouldn't let in! I recognize your boots. They had yellow laces and two eyelets were missing!"

Mrs. Flood's cousin started for the door, but two men grabbed him. In the scuffle, a gold pocket watch tumbled to the floor.

"Pap's watch!" one of the men shouted. He popped open its lid, revealing an inscription: "Wm. Honecker, 1880."

The cousin and his accomplices were hanged. From that time forward, Papa never left home without arranging for two of our hired men to stay in the house.

* * *

One day Maud Flood asked me how it felt to come so close.

"Close to what?" I asked her.

"You know," she said, and drew a finger across her throat. "You know what criminals do to women."

I couldn't believe she would joke about such a thing. "I pray you never have to go through what Mama and Ola and I did," I said.

Whirling around, she marched away. But she was right: the unspeakable had visited us that night. My world had darkened.

PAPA IN POLITICS

One day around 1908, Papa happened to be in Minerva, our county seat, eating dinner at Mrs. Crigler's hotel. Five of the town's leading citizens, all a generation older than he was, came to ask him if he would run for County Clerk. The incumbent, Billy Counts, a Democrat, was a drunkard. Responsible men like Papa's five friends, who were all Democrat, not only wanted Billy Counts out of office, but would go to a lot of trouble to get him out.

"Who? Me?" Papa laughed. "In *this* county?"

Mr. Hugh Mayes laid a hand on Papa's shoulder. "All of us will support you. You'll have a good chance," he said. "If there's ever going to be a year for a Republican to get into office, this is it. We've talked it over. You're the man to do it, Jack."

All these men were enough older than Papa to have been his father. Captain Riley, a man in his sixties, had fought in the Confederate cavalry. Captain McComas had been an officer in the Confederate Army under General Lee. Captain McComas said, "Think about it, Jack. It won't be easy, but with our help you can do it."

The best advice Papa ever heard about marriage had come from Captain McComas, so he listened seriously to what he had to say.

As a young, newly married man, Captain McComas had helped his wife with small chores around the house. He was deeply in love with her and enjoyed surprising her by filling her wood box, or replenishing the hot-water reservoir of her cook stove, or cleaning out her flour safe. It had been like a game to him, he told Papa: he loved to see the look of pleasure and gratitude in her eyes. "When you're young and in love," Captain McComas said, "just doing little jobs like that, and seeing the light in the eye of your girl, is a wonderful thing!"

"But one day it dawned on me that Becky had changed from being surprised to expecting my help, and even depending on me. I found myself resenting it. One morning, I sat shelling beans, a small job I'd offered to do while she attended to something else. I realized that outside in the streets of Minerva, on the steps of the courthouse, at the bank, and at my own store, leaders of the community were making important decisions–without me!"

"There I sat, a grown man, the head of this household, in that attic, pounding beans out of their shells. It was an easy job any boy would be glad to do for twenty-five cents, when I should be out doing something worthwhile," he told Papa. "And, Jack, I threw that maul across the floor as far as I could, ran down and kissed Becky, and told her I was through wasting my time with little jobs that she could hire a boy to do."

Every now and then, Papa surprised Mama by doing one of her chores. Not enough that she ever expected it, but just enough to brighten her day.

Mama's reaction to the news that Papa had decided to run for County Clerk was about what he expected: "Oh, Jack! In this county? Captain McComas? Mr. Hugh Mays? Mr. Ed MacArthur? Mr. Bainbridge? Captain Riley? Why would *they* back a Republican?"

"*You* married *me*," Papa reminded her.

I don't think Papa had made up his mind about running for office until Mama began to argue that he couldn't win. "I might just have a chance, Carrie," he reasoned.

"How can you," she countered, "when you know, even my own family wouldn't vote for you?"

This was true. Her uncles had fought for the Confederacy. They had been so upset at the outcome, that they'd emigrated to Arkansas. Mama's family liked Papa well enough–admired him in fact, and were pleased that Mama had married him–but the Civil War had ended just forty years before, and wounds still ran deep. Confederate Reunions were held every year, not far from our farm. There was never a reunion of Union veterans. Feelings ran especially deep in a border state like West Virginia.

* * *

My brothers and sisters and I soon found out what it could be like, in our part of the world, to have a Republican father running for office. The moment our schoolmates saw us, they lined up along the schoolhouse fence, flapped their arms, and crowed like roosters. Roosters were the emblem of the Democratic Party in those days. I was thirteen, Dayton was eleven, Hugh nine, Bess and Lily younger still. When we arrived in our carryall on a school morning, to give some of these friends a lift to school, they were polite enough until we got there. Then they began. We pretended we didn't care. "They're just teasing," I whispered to my brothers and sisters.

One morning, after Papa had begun to actively campaign, one of the older Waybright boys said, "Your pa came to see our pa to ask for his vote, but our pa said he'd never give it."

Six-year-old Oatie Kelly told my brother Hugh, "If your pa was a Democrat, my pa would vote for him." Oatie's father, a moonshiner, couldn't sign his own name.

"My uncle would vote for your dad if he was a Democrat," Willie Hazzard had the nerve to say. He was the son of one of our washerwomen.

Every morning, the gauntlet of flapping, crowing, Democratic roosters lined up at the schoolhouse fence. Our closest friends, the Flood children, and their cousins, the Hunters, the Neff children, the Kefavers, even the Waybrights, flapped their arms and crowed at us. Even our teachers, who we had believed liked us, never once interfered with the teasing.

* * *

In any event, Papa did get some Democratic votes. He carried the precinct of Chinkapin Creek, which meant that Mama had been wrong about her family, or about at least some of her cousins. With the help of his five older Democratic friends, Papa carried the county seat, eleven miles away, and the Upper Fork, a Republican pocket where his people had originally come from. He carried even Mount Hebron and the Sinks. Yet even before the polls closed, unpleasant stories came back to us. One was about Mama's own first cousin, Porter Cody, standing on the steps of Mr. Waybright's carpenter shop, which served as the polling place. He announced, "I don't give a damn how many Codys vote for Jack Wister, here's one won't and ain't ashamed to tell it!"

"Porter owes you money, Jack," said Mama when she heard that. "That makes him sore-headed."

Over all, Papa lost Guthrie County. After the polls closed and the vote had been added up, Billy Counts' backers produced the key to the room in the County Courthouse where they'd locked him up so the voters wouldn't see him drunk on election day. They carried him out to celebrate.

The count was 105 for Billy Counts, 72 for Papa. Women didn't vote in those days. The voting age was twenty-one. There was a poll tax, so poor people couldn't vote.

The race had been close enough to encourage Papa to try again.

I forget whether his next opportunity came in 1910 or 1912. "I really think I have a chance this time, Carrie," he told Mama. "Remember, a lot of good Democrats voted for me in 1908." The post he aimed at this time was Sheriff. In 1908 in Hardwicke County, another Democratic stronghold, Papa's brother had won the race for Coroner, on the Republican ticket. Papa considered this a good sign.

Papa's adversary in his second race was another incompetent Democrat whom Captain McComas and his friends hoped to unseat. As before, we Wister children suffered unmerciful teasing by our contemporaries. As before, Papa was defeated, again by a close margin.

He hated campaigning, and considered his cause lost. He never again ran for elected office. He did, however, hold posts handed out by the State's Republican administration. They were of the sort that, at the federal level, had gone to other Republicans such as Mrs. Lowry, our postmistress, whose brother had fought for the Union. In 1909, a Republican governor appointed Papa to the State Board of Regents, renewing an appointment given him in 1901 by an earlier Republican governor. The County Court, which must surely have been Democrat, appointed him Commissioner of the County Farm, and Judge Kump appointed him Jury Commissioner for four years.

Before Papa's day, a Republican administration had awarded his father, our Grandpa Wister, the post of Deputy Commissioner of Internal Revenue for Eastern West Virginia. A subsequent Republican administration appointed Papa to the same job.

These appointments must have consoled him, up to a point. They came without the humiliating need to run for office. It was certainly a relief for my brothers and sisters and me, and for Mama, as well.

I Make A Trip

When I was 9 years old, I took my first trip from the farm to a big city: Martinsburg, West Virginia.

I had never been farther away from home than Minerva, our county seat, eleven miles away. Martinsburg, where Papa worked part of the year, was a hundred and fifty miles from Chinkapin Creek, two and a half days' travel by stage and train. My Uncle Ike accompanied me, and I stayed with my Uncle Pent and Aunt Edith.

Mama and I drove to Mr. Armistead's store. We chose a length of Navy blue ducking for my traveling dress, a length of blue plaid gingham, two lengths of dimity, and one of flowered organdie. We also chose matching grosgrain ribbon for tying up my pigtails. The next day, our hired man Reuben drove me, along with the material and the McCall patterns Mama used to make all my dresses, to Grandma Cody's.

Under any circumstances, I loved going to Grandma's. Soon she and I were at work, cutting and basting the ducking to make a sailor dress. My Aunt Nan, a flighty, undependable girl my age, watched. When we had finished the sailor dress, we made one of plaid gingham. Then we tackled the dimity and organdie. These last had many tucks and flounces. Grandma and I also made me a few pieces of underwear.

Mama ordered a "Boston shopping bag" from Sears & Roebuck. Made of soft dark brown leather, with a drawstring closure, it was big enough to hold my pocketbook and gloves, a supply of handkerchiefs, and a sandwich for my first day on the road.

I wore a sailor hat of rough cream-colored straw, banded around the crown with a broad navy-blue ribbon that ended in streamers down my back.

"Nellie, be sure to come back the way you are," Reuben said. "Don't put on airs the way some do when they go away from home."

On the morning I was to leave, Mrs. Pennybacker, our housekeeper, packed for me. As she bent down to kiss me goodbye, she slipped a new linen handkerchief into my pocketbook. Mamma kissed me and waved me off. A farewell party of my brothers and sisters accompanied me down the yard.

The stage was supposed to pass our gate around eight in the morning, but that day it was late. My brown oxfords pinched my feet. The sun grew hot. Mama sat up on the porch, rocking the baby's cradle with her foot, and winding a ball of red yarn in her hands. At last, a cloud of dust and the jangle of harness announced the coming of the stage.

The stage had three double seats. The first was occupied by the driver and the mail sacks; the other two were empty. Mr. Riddle, the driver, was also our mail carrier every other day. A cap and loose-fitting coat framed his grim, weathered face. He did not look at me as he said, "Going somewhere, young lady?" My brothers and I were too small to boost Mama's brown grip up into the stage. Mr. Riddle gave it a glum look, eased himself down and took it from us. I climbed in, he climbed back to his seat, and we were off.

No one was out at Floods', or at Neffs', or Morgans', to see me go flying by. Mr. John Morgan, who on any usual day would have been out chopping wood, was nowhere in sight. No loafers were on the porch at the store by the schoolhouse.

At the Chinkapin Creek post office, the stage drew to a halt. There stood Uncle Ike. He was Grandma Cody's brother, a small man with a grey, neatly clipped Van Dyke beard. He always dressed exactly the same: a dark suit, white shirt, loosely knotted black string tie, and creased felt hat. He owned a burr mill, and was a justice of the peace. Everyone called him "Squire McCue."

Mrs. Lowery, the postmistress, and her daughter Miss Belle, waved from the post office doorway. "Remember us to everyone!" they said. Miss Belle's sister had married one of my uncles, and lived in Martinsburg. As I sat on my perch up on the stage seat next to Uncle Ike, I felt included in an inner circle, all of whose members had been to Martinsburg. Soon I would be there too. With a jangling of the harness, the stage was off.

No one was out at Uncle Vergil's. No one was out at Grandma's or at Uncle H's. Would my cousin Mary see me go by? We rattled past without seeing a soul.

By now a fine yellow dust covered my new dress and oxfords. We passed the mouth of the Big Gap, and clattered over the iron bridge. A few small farms followed. I had never been so far. At each farmhouse, Mr. Riddle stopped the stage. He got down, limped to the mailbox to yank out the empty canvas mail sack, and shove in a full one. A sign over the door of one of stops read, "Weedy Run Post Office." Mr. Riddle said, "Want to get down and stretch your legs?" Uncle Ike and I went into the post office while the horses were changed. It was noon. We had covered seven miles.

I was surprised to see a familiar face in the post office. It was Mr. Riggleman, who sometimes came to our house.

"Sam, this is my great-niece Nellie," said Uncle Ike.

"Why, howdy do, young lady." Mr. Riggleman clearly didn't recognize me, but he called into the back of the house, "Bessie, look who's here!"

A middle-aged woman appeared in the doorway. "Why, I declare, if it isn't Squire McCue," she said. She looked at me. "And who's this?"

"This is my great-niece, Nellie." Uncle Ike sat down. I rummaged in my Boston shopping bag for the cold cornbread. Uncle Ike and I sat on straight chairs in the half of the Rigglemans' front room, which served as post office and waiting room for the stage. As we ate, Mrs. Riggleman came in with glasses of cold buttermilk.

The stage made two more stops, one at a little post office called Daisy and one at Flats. At each stop, Mr. Riddle muttered, "Want to get down and stretch your legs?"

By the time we crossed the river, the sun had moved from the right side of the stage to the left, and it was late afternoon. All told, we had covered nineteen miles when we arrived in Vestal to spend the night.

Mr. Riddle's house, which served as a stage stop, was a big ramshackle dirty white building. It opened directly onto the dirt street. Uncle Ike and I were his only guests. Mrs. Riddle, a small, timid woman, showed me my room. Downstairs, Uncle Ike produced from his pockets a copy of the *South Branch Review,* our county paper. "Why don't you go visit your great-aunt Becky?" he suggested, giving the paper a shake. "Mrs. Riddle will get someone to show you where she lives."

My heart sank. I didn't want to go looking in a strange place for a great-aunt I didn't know. But, already, Mrs. Riddle was calling toward the back of the house, "Sam! Sam! Come show this young lady where Mrs. Abel Parks lives."

A boy of about my age appeared in a doorway. He looked me over without enthusiasm. "Well, come on," he mumbled.

Sam walked a dozen paces ahead of me, making sure that no one he knew would get the idea he had anything to do with me. In case I should attempt to talk to him, he dragged a stick over the paling fences that lined the board-walk, making a deafening clatter. In this hostile Indian file, he and I approached a corner.

"There 'tis," he said, pointing to the left. He turned and clattered off the way we had come.

Great-aunt Becky looked like Grandpa Cody, as if his large grey eyes had been transposed onto a woman's face. "Well, well," she said, "so you're Charley's grandchild. Come on in."

"Your uncle's at the farm today," she added, as if I knew what farm she meant. "He'll be real sorry to miss you." She gave me a glass of milk and a ginger cookie. "And how are your folks?" she asked, "and how's your grandpa?"

* * *

Suppose something had happened to Uncle Ike? What if the stage left early? What if I couldn't find my way back to Mr. Riddle's house?

I had taken care to memorize the houses Sam and I had passed. Soon, proud and excited to have found my way alone, I was back at the stage stop.

Supper was served on a big table, with lots of small children around. I felt right at home. Mrs. Riddle served the kind of food I was used to, home-cured ham fried with milk gravy, light-bread, hominy, snap beans, and early lettuce. The ham was so much like what we had at home, I thought it *was* ours. Papa sold hams to the two hotels in Minerva. He must have sold them in Vestal as well. At the meal, and afterward, Sam was nowhere to be seen. The next morning at breakfast, he wasn't present either. This pleased me as much as I expect it pleased him.

A different stage took Uncle Ike and me to Keyser. Our new driver was a pimply fellow called John. We had a fellow-passenger, a young man who, as soon as he sat down, began to talk. "Look at that bull yonder in that field," he said. "Look at that barn. Now there's a fine stand of chestnuts up against that hill. Lightning sure took the top out of that pin oak. Good roads in through here, mighty good. My, it's hot."

Three road wagons, topped by box-like structures, stopped to let us go by. I studied these with interest. I knew that Armistead's store, at home, received supplies by just such wagons from Keyser. Might these wagons be destined for Mr. Armistead's? Buggies and men on horseback passed us. We passed a lady riding sidesaddle.

Our horses were changed again at Burlington, at noon. A little inn there, which also housed the post office, gave us dinner which, again, seemed familiar: ham and gravy, beans and light-bread. An old man dozed in a corner. The talkative young man shared our table. "Look at the boards in this floor," he said. "Look at that doorframe. Looky at his dish here." Soon after eating, we were on our way again.

The Reynolds Hotel was a dirty brown building, which occupied a corner facing the Baltimore & Ohio Railroad depot. Uncle Ike took care, now that we were to stay in a big-city hotel, to assure me that his room was right next to mine.

From my window overlooking the depot, I saw miles of tracks. I thought, "some of those trains must go all the way to Baltimore!" Perhaps the locomotive I saw was part of the train Uncle Ike and I would board in the morning.

"I do believe you're enjoying yourself, Nellie!" Uncle Ike said.

The dining room in the Reynolds Hotel was very different from Mrs. Crigler's little dining room in Minerva. There were tables for four or six. With Uncle Ike and me were a middle-aged man in a yellow suit, two grey-haired men wearing dark suits like Uncle Ike's and, what excited me, a railroad employee in a blue uniform. I was the only child, the only female. I was having my first meal in a real hotel, in a real town! I don't remember what we ate, or whether it was good. I can't remember if it was on the table when we sat down or if somebody brought it. I remember a sideboard, a cupboard and Uncle Ike saying again, "I do believe you're enjoying yourself, Nellie!"

Long before the rest of the hotel was stirring, I was up, washed, dressed, and at my window. *Where* could all those trains be going? What were they carrying? As I watched, a great string of cars, loaded with logs, came backing down the tracks.

My first impression of the interior of a train was of plush red upholstery. "This car is for passengers going all the way to Baltimore," Uncle Ike said, as he and I walked on through to the coaches.

The jerk-jerk-jerk of the train, the stuffy air, and the trees and fields moving past the sealed dusty windows made me feel at first queasy, then distinctly uncomfortable. Uncle Ike tried to raise the sash. "Close your eyes, Nellie," he said. A voice called, "Piedmont, all off for Piedmont," and, "Cumberland, next stop Cumberland!"

I obeyed. All the way to Martinsburg, sixty miles or more, I kept my eyes closed, only opening them when I heard a voice say, "Tickets, please," or when Uncle Ike announced, "We're in Maryland, Nellie!" and then, "Now we're back in West Virginia!" Each time the train stopped, I looked out and saw a different dusty depot. Some had people standing on the platform; some had men in railroad uniforms walking along, peering under the cars. As I began to feel better, the locomotive gave a jerk, and I closed my eyes again. At last I heard a voice say, "Martinsburg!" My uncle nudged me. "Look, Nellie."

Negro cabins flew by the window. I saw mills, quarries, sheds, and factories. The train slowed, and a platform came into view. On the other side stood another train, filled with people. People seemed to be everywhere. And there was Papa!

"Poor Nellie," Papa said. "I see you don't care for train travel."

A hack took us from the station. I had never heard so much noise: of voices, of horse's hooves, of wheels on paved streets. I had never seen so many buildings. Martinsburg, an industrial town with hot and smoky air, seemed ugly to me.

We entered quieter streets. I saw churches. The streets widened and the houses became bigger. At last the hack stopped, in front of a broad white front porch and many tall bay windows. We had arrived.

Of the trip home, the train ride and the stage, I remember little. But I remember how Chinkapin Creek had shrunk while I was gone, how small the rooms in our old house seemed, how low the ceilings were, and how worn and plain the furniture.

Yet it was wonderful to be back with Mama and my brothers and sisters and to smell the familiar odors of home.

"I see you took my advice, Nellie," said Reuben. "You haven't put on airs."

THE CEMETERY

When Miz Fan Wister died, her husband Amos asked Papa if he could bury her in one of the two graveyards on our farm. Amos was a distant cousin of Papa's. Papa said yes, of course. Miz Fan, of an older generation, had been a friend. Born Hamrick, Miz Fan was descended from old settlers. Mr. Amos, who had moved to Chinkapin Creek from Back Mill Creek, had no family graveyard.

Papa rode up the mountain to mark a place for Miz Fan. It was June, but spring had come late, and there had been a lot of rain. Water still drained off the mountain. With every step Bashaw took, his hooves sank deep into the mud.

A corner of the old graveyard, next to an angle in the old iron fence, seemed a good place for Miz Fan. Papa sat in the saddle, looking at the old graves. He asked himself, not for the first time, how the land drained. A second graveyard, started when Grandpa Wister bought our farm, was within sight. Below both graveyards was our spring, which supplied the neighboring Flood family farm, as well as our own. The Floods also had two old burying grounds on their property, both occupying part of this same high bench of land.

For years, Papa had suspected that burying people in these graveyards might have something to do with typhoid epidemics. He asked himself in what way infection might be carried underground. Many graveyards were situated on farms around Chinkapin Creek. The oldest, like ours, were always on high ground, probably because the living had wanted to enjoy the view when they went up there to tend the graves.

As Papa rode back down across our broad pasture-field, he said suddenly, to no one in particular—to Bashaw perhaps, "We ought to have a community cemetery in Chinkapin Creek."

That evening it rained. The next morning, when they lowered Miz Fan's coffin into the muddy grave, they heard a splash at the bottom. The hay in the fields, bent and matted, was rotting.

My little brothers asked Mama many questions about Miz Fan's death. She was the first dead person they had ever seen. They wanted to know where she had gone. The burying itself preoccupied them. This was a woman they had known all their lives. How could we now bury her in the dirt? After the ceremony, they decided to go up and look at her grave. Dayton was eight, Hugh a year younger. They saw that a crack had opened around the new grave, where fresh dirt ought to have joined tightly to the grassy edge. Dayton found a long stick, got down on his hands and knees and poked the stick into the crack. He and Hugh heard a hollow thud as the stick struck Miz Fan's coffin.

That evening at supper, Hugh said, "Papa, Dayton touched Miz Fan's coffin."

Papa looked at Dayton. "And how did you do that?" After my brothers explained, Papa exchanged a thoughtful look with Mama.

The next morning, Papa rode up to the graveyard with a shovel. The damp dirt over Miz Fan's grave shone raw against the green grass and dewberry vines. The crack the boys had described was an inch wide. He dismounted and shoveled dirt into the crack. When he was done, only a hard dirt seal, trampled shiny by Papa's boots, remained where the crack had been.

A small cedar grew just outside the fence. Papa stared a while at this cedar, then dug it up and planted it inside the graveyard. Other small cedars grew around the hillside. He dug up two more, and carried them to the second grave-yard. Inside the board fence, where more graves might have been dug, Papa planted the cedars. When he had finished, he said to himself, "Those cedars will grow into big trees and fill in all the empty space. We've got to establish a community cemetery in Chinkapin Creek."

Papa knew where a cemetery might be situated. Not on our farm, as we were too far outside Chinkapin Creek. Mr. Saul McComas owned land right on a pretty knoll with locusts, scrub oaks and wild cherries growing thickly all around. It overlooked no wells or springs. When Papa approached him, Mr. McComas said, "I always wanted to move my people from Bath County, Jack. A cemetery in Chinkapin Creek will give me an excuse to do it. I'll donate the land."

He and Papa walked the length of the knoll. They came to Mr. Hugh Caudle's line fence. "Maybe Hugh will sell us some of his land," Papa said.

Mr. Caudle agreed.

Mr. McComas, as the major land donor, got first choice of the lots. He chose a spot looking toward his house. Soon everyone was buying lots in the new cemetery. It turned out that many people in Chinkapin Creek had shared Papa's concerns about drainage from the old graveyards.

Not long after the inauguration of the cemetery, one of our frequent typhoid epidemics broke out. Within weeks, the new cemetery had its first graves. Later that year, when we had an outbreak of diphtheria, which affected mostly children, new small graves were added. These tragedies led to a rush by families to buy lots and move bodies from the old hilltop graveyards.

Uncle Vergil, Mama's brother, came to Mama about moving bodies from the McCue graveyard.

Mama replied in such a tone of pain that I looked over at her. "Oh, Vergil," she said, "there's nothing left there to be moved!"

"Mary Alice wants it," Uncle Vergil insisted.

One day not long afterward, I saw Uncle Vergil and his hired man go by our lane, driving a wagon. Soon they came back and stopped. Uncle Vergil got down and came into the house.

"You were right, Carrie," he told Mama. "All we found were some of those little metal handles. We're moving them anyhow."

Mama looked at him curiously. Vergil seemed to know what she was thinking.

"There were..." Vergil continued, "some...bones. We're moving them, too."

Mama touched his hand.

"Mary Alice will be able to see our four babies in the new cemetery," Uncle Vergil said. "She can walk there sometimes."

When I saw the four little graves in Uncle Vergil's lot in the new cemetery, I thought about Aunt Mary Alice. Though she and Uncle Vergil had been married for as long as I could remember, they had no living children. All had died in infancy.

Then, as if moving the dead had changed something, she and Uncle Vergil started having healthy babies, one after the other.

Floods moved everybody out of their graveyard, except one old grave of a Mr. Schrader, who had been a preacher in the Northern Methodist church. No one knew how he'd gotten there. Maybe, when he died, no one had known where else to put him. Maybe Mr. Flood, the only local Methodist at the time, had offered a place.

Mrs. Flood said, about Mr. Schrader, "We'll leave him where he lies."

One day a stranger came to our door. A small man with a Van Dyke beard, he was not young. "I'm Merle Schrader," he said. "I hear you-all have a cemetery here now. I want to move my grandpa."

When she heard this, Mrs. Flood said, "For a man who never even bothered to take his grandpa home, he's mighty interested in him now."

The same idlers, who'd gone to Floods' to watch the digging up of the old graves, came back to watch the moving of Mr. Schrader. The diggers got down to Mr. Schrader's coffin, passed ropes underneath it, as usual, and tied the ropes to a team of horses. They were surprised to find that the coffin couldn't be moved.

Someone said, "there's bound to be something in there besides Mr. Schrader." Everyone looked at Mr. Schrader's grandson, whose family had let his grandfather be buried in a strange place, yet was now so interested in moving him.

The audience looked back at Mr. Schrader's coffin.

"How long has he been here, do you reckon?" said Bax Flood, who had helped with the digging.

"He preached at Cecil Arbogasts's funeral," said an oldtimer.

Nobody there remembered Cecil Arbogast.

"Somebody go get an auger," said Dr. Cody.

Charley Flood ran down the mountain to his mother's barn for an auger.

The group waited. No one said a word. Soon Charley came panting back and handed the auger to Dr. Cody. Everyone crowded close, as Dr. Cody climbed down into the grave. They heard the dull grind of the auger boring into sodden wood. Suddenly there was a gushing sound, and a stream of dark water spurted up.

Dr. Cody, wet all over, scrambled out of the grave. They drilled a second hole on the side near the bottom. When the water finally stopped draining, the men lifted up a coffin so light that it seemed Mr. Schrader himself must have trickled out. When, at the insistence of Mr. Schrader's grandson, they opened the coffin, it was clear that most of him had. The younger Schrader looked deflated.

Mr. Schrader's coffin was loaded into Floods' spring wagon. Mr. Schrader's grandson climbed into his buggy and set off behind it. The little procession wound down the hillside through Floods' pastures, down toward the road and the new cemetery.

When Papa heard the story about moving Mr. Schrader, he said, "Thank heaven we now have a cemetery."

Mrs. Flood said, "What do you expect that little fellow with the pointy beard thought he was going to find?"

ROBERT E. LEE KILGORE

I'm not sure how our family happened to own a blacksmith shop. An ancient building made of logs, it had a forge where our hired men shod horses and mended machinery. It stood near the line fence at the far end of our calf lot, as far as a building could be from our house and outbuildings, in case of fire. The warped old door hung ajar. In the dusty interior, my little brothers and I climbed onto the enormous stone hearth, pumped the leather bellows–or tried to—and hammered on the anvil. We had no resident blacksmith.

Papa hoped a blacksmith would settle among us. The town of Minerva, eleven miles away, had two smiths, brothers who worked together. Papa and our neighbors had to make long trips for repairs which only skilled smiths could manage.

One day, when Papa had business in Minerva, he noticed a new blacksmith's shop. He thought to himself, "this fellow's going to have a hard time. The McKendrick brothers don't leave any smithing undone in this town; maybe this man will be the one for *us*."

The newcomer was small and swarthy, with coarse, Indian-black hair. His hands, for a small man, were large and obviously strong, and he had the powerfully developed forearms all smiths have. Papa watched him mend a broken hame, and was impressed by his serious manner and obvious skill. The stranger had tidily arranged the shop itself, a former stable. Instead of the usual clutter of dusty old wagon wheels, singletrees, and trace chains, the space was scrupulously clean. All the while that Papa stood in the doorway watching, the new smith didn't once look up, though he must have been aware he was being watched.

At Mr. Eddie Sanderson's general store, Papa asked what was known about the new blacksmith.

"I can't say what kind of work he does because everybody here uses McKendricks'," Mr. Eddie said. "I know he's from the Valley somewhere. I hear he married one of the Evicks."

By "the Valley", Mr. Eddie meant the Shenandoah, which lay close by to the east. Evick was an old and honorable name there. Evicks had been among its earliest settlers, though, by my father's day, their bloodline had run a little thin. The average Minerva resident of that time wouldn't have considered marriage to one of them to be a step up the social ladder.

That same day, Papa made a point of stopping by the shop again and introducing himself. "I live in Chinkapin Creek, eleven miles up the river," he said. "We need a blacksmith there."

The small man glanced at Papa. Without a word or even acknowledgment, he went back to work.

Each time Papa had business in Minerva, he made a point of passing by the new smith's. Each time, he saw the newcomer sitting idle in the doorway. Papa had been right, of course: there wasn't enough work in the town for a third smith.

One day in Chinkapin Creek, he noticed a sign nailed to a small cabin at the end of Waybrights' lane. It read, "R. E. L. KILGORE, BLACKSMITH."

Papa felt responsible for Mr. Kilgore's being there, so he hired him to do a job for us. The next morning, Mr. Kilgore walked the two miles, because he had no horse, and arrived at our farm before daylight.

West Virginia produces coal, but the use of coal wasn't common in our part of the state, except by blacksmiths. We knew he had arrived because of the unusual odor that drifted up from the direction of the blacksmith shop. At breakfast, there sat the new smith, eating steadily with his black eyes fixed on his plate, saying not a word. Only once did he glance up in an odd way, like a man disoriented, checking where he was.

After he had gone back to work, Mama said, "Jack, that poor man has the saddest face I ever saw."

Word spread that Mr. Kilgore did good work for us, and soon he had as many jobs as he could handle. His wife and daughter lived with him in a tiny house behind his shop. His daughter was blond and blue-eyed and had sweet, delicate features. She sat behind me at school. No one ever saw Mrs. Kilgore, not even in the yard of their house. At recess, on days when my friends and I went to admire the display of coffins in Mr. Waybright's carpentry shop window, I noticed that the Kilgores' little house looked abandoned.

Mama's policy was not to let me go to other girls' houses. She feared what I might learn from too much "loose talk." Yet she liked me to bring friends to our home. Soon, Alma Kilgore was spending nights at our house. "Her mother must be very nice," Mama said. "She has such good manners."

But Ginny Hamrick, who came early on Mondays to do our washing, said, "Mr. Kilgore he drinks and beats Mrs. Kilgore."

Mama frowned at Ginny. Mama didn't permit gossip in our house, so Ginny said nothing more. I soon forgot the story. I liked Mr. Kilgore, who let my brothers and me watch him work. On afternoons when, home from school, we saw coal smoke pouring from the chimney of our old blacksmith shop, we stopped by to watch him work. He never spoke to us, but only went on with his job. We felt at home in his presence, perhaps because he had become familiar. We felt we had known him a long time.

At hog butchering time, Mr. Kilgore asked Mama if he could buy fresh jowl. She let him have something she rarely allowed anyone outside our family: newly made sausage. "He works so hard," she said, watching him carry away the brown paper-wrapped package. In addition to the sausage, she'd slipped in a heart, a liver, and sweetbreads. "He has such a sad face."

I believe Mama made a point of being kind to Mr. Kilgore, to make up for the mean things people said about him. By that time we'd heard from others that he drank and beat Mrs. Kilgore.

At the end of the school year, Alma and I were chosen by our teachers to recite poems. The custom was for these poems to be said at the final exercises, not by those about to graduate, but by younger pupils. Alma and I were ten years old. I wore a favorite blue dress and matching bows on my pigtails. Alma's dress, made for her by her mother, was also blue, and she also wore blue hair ribbons. First Alma, then I recited. As we walked back through the small audience to resume our seats, Teenie Hardesty leaned into

the aisle and whispered, "Nellie, I liked your piece and the way you said it."

Beside Teenie sat a thin woman wearing a long dark coat. Teenie turned to her and added, "Alma said hers nice too, Mrs. Kilgore." The woman smiled thinly at Teenie. She then directed at me a look which I have since tried to analyze. It was so laden with frustration, anger, and resentment that I feel, to this day, as sobered as if she had slapped me. Her eyes rested on me only an instant, but the fires that burned there seared an impression that smoldered throughout the rest of the ceremony. Sharing an honor with my friend had given me a feeling of joy, which then withered away, once I'd seen her mother's expression.

Ginny Hamrick reported to us that Mrs. Kilgore had had a third baby. "Something's wrong with it," Ginny said. "*She's* sick too."

Mama drove the buggy to the tiny house, carrying two blackberry pies and a big piece of ham. She found Mrs. Kilgore in bed, and the baby in a cradle beside the wood box. Something *was* wrong with it. It never cried once. Mama changed the baby's linens and tidied the small house. Mrs. Kilgore said nothing. "All things work together for good for them that love God and keep His commandments," she told Mrs. Kilgore. It was a passage which had comforted her at troubled times in her own life. Mrs. Kilgore showed no response; she only looked away.

One day Papa came home and reported, "Carrie, Mr. Kilgore has asked me to help him put the new baby in the State Hospital in Huntington."

"Oh, no, Jack!" replied Mama.

Mr. Kilgore had turned to my father because he was Commissioner of the Poor and a member of the County

Court. Papa arranged for the baby to go to the State Hospital. Soon, with Mr. Kilgore driving our new Ford, he, Papa and the infant, headed west on a long trip to the other side of the state. Within weeks of their return, the hospital phoned Papa to report that the baby had died.

Ginny Hamrick had never dared talk back to Mama, but one morning she looked directly at Mama and said, "That's *true*, Mrs. Wister. Mr. Kilgore he *does* beat Mrs. Kilgore."

Alma and her mother disappeared from Chinkapin Creek.

As for Mr. Kilgore himself, he stopped working. He promised Papa to come to us, but he would arrive on the wrong day, or he'd forget entirely. It seemed possible that he did indeed drink, It seemed possible, too, that he might have beaten Mrs. Kilgore. As I passed his shop, I saw him sitting in the open doorway. His powerful hands hung idle between his skinny knees, and his intense black eyes stared into the dusty lane.

I missed Alma. Where had she and Mrs. Kilgore gone? Back to the Valley? I felt sure Alma would write to me.

One day, the new blacksmith shop stood closed and empty. Papa asked Mr. Waybright about Mr. Kilgore. No one had any idea where he had gone.

Several years later, during a summer when I was home from boarding school, I drove to the Valley with Papa on a cattle-buying trip. We stopped in Monterey, Virginia. There, we saw a man who looked enough like Mr. Kilgore to be his twin.

"Would you happen to be kin to a Robert E. Lee Kilgore?" Papa asked him.

"He's my brother," said the man. "*Was*," he amended. "He used to live over in West Virginia. Then he come back here. But he never stayed. I don't know what become of him."

"He was a good smith," said Papa.

"I'll give you that," said Mr. Kilgore's brother. "But nobody needs a smith these days. Nowadays, these here automobiles are all the thing."

Another man had joined Papa and Mr. Kilgore's brother, and was listening to the conversation. He gave Papa an appraising look. "He's in jail," he said. Then he added, "He killed his wife, mister."

I was shocked! I walked away, out of earshot, knowing Papa would not want me to hear more.

When Papa rejoined me, he said Mr. Kilgore had indeed killed his wife. No one knew why. He was in jail in Harrisonburg. No one knew what had become of Alma.

In the nineteen-thirties I was living in the southwestern part of the state and had two small children. One day I passed the local hospital, and there on the front steps stood a familiar figure.

"Nellie?" she asked me.

"Alma!"

I hardly knew what to say. It had been a lifetime since she and I had recited our poems at the school exercises in Chinkapin Creek. I told her my own news: I'd finished school and held a job as a teacher in Monroe County. I'd married a man from that part of the state and had two small children.

She studied my face, then looked away. "I guess you know about Mother."

I said I had heard something.

She wouldn't look at me. "Dad died," she whispered. "The electric chair. Maybe you knew that?"

A silence fell between us.

"Now I'm married, like you." She looked at me again. We exchanged addresses and promised to write.

I wrote to Alma. She answered. That Christmas we exchanged cards. The following year, as if by tacit agreement, neither of us sent cards. I never saw her again.

Aunt Edith

I never liked my Aunt Edith. Whenever she spoke to anyone, she never looked them in the eye, but stared at a point about in the middle of their forehead. On a summer day in 1904, Papa, Uncle Ike, and I arrived at her big house in Martinsburg, West Virginia. She opened the door and, without a word of welcome, stared at Papa's forehead. "Dr. Wister is busy, but he'll be here for dinner," she said.

"Dr. Wister" was her husband. He was Papa's brother, my uncle. Aunt Edith's own father stood at the door with us.

Very old ladies in those days spoke of their husbands as "Mr. So-and-So" and addressed them that way to their faces. I knew for a fact, however, that Aunt Edith was only thirty-seven years old, because I'd heard Mama say so.

"Your cousin Ann can show you your room, Nellie," said Aunt Edith, as she turned from Papa's forehead to mine. She talked so fast it was hard to follow her. Sometimes, in the middle of a sentence, she changed her mind about what her subject was. She had other peculiar habits. When her doorbell rang, she'd change her dress before answering it. She could change from one shirtwaist and skirt to another quicker than most women can tie their aprons. The hot summer afternoon that Papa and Uncle Ike and I arrived, I'm sure she changed into her starched white shirtwaist and black skirt when she heard our horses' hooves arriving in the street.

Aunt Edith set her dinner table as if it were Sunday, with a heavy white damask cloth, elaborately monogrammed silverware, and a big cut-glass bowl with silver edges, filled with dahlias. I thought she did this especially for our arrival, but the next morning her table was set in exactly the same way, except zinnias, instead of the dahlias, were in a china bowl with roses painted on it. She kept every part of her house looking as if at any moment she expected company. That first day she served us fresh beefsteak. Being a farm girl, I wondered who would butcher beef in August? I searched Papa's face for a clue but he was talking to my uncle.

Then she served us ice cream! At home, we had ice cream only at my grandparents' house on Christmas Day. But ice cream and fresh beef were common all year round in Martinsburg.

At Aunt Edith's I had my first ground-beef patty and my first coddled egg. Bananas were a rare treat for a farm girl. Aunt Edith kept a basket of them in the pantry, where every day I made a point of checking on them. They were to be eaten by anyone who wanted one, so I did.

Our old farmhouse, considered large, seemed modest compared to Aunt Edith's tall dwelling, with its high ceilings. The first floor had a pair of parlors, a dining room, a serving pantry, a storage pantry, and three rooms used by Uncle Pent for his medical offices. In the basement were still more pantries, a vast kitchen, and what Aunt Edith called a "laundry"–a new word for me; we had a wash house on our farm. Aunt Edith's second floor consisted of nine bedrooms, one for herself and Uncle Pent, one for each of my five cousins, one for Papa, one for Uncle Ike, and one for me. On the third floor were rooms for Aunt Edith's hired girls—"maids," she called them. One she called "the cook."

Uncle Pent's carriage house was in the process of being converted into a "garage"—another new word. "Gare-ridge," my cousins assured me it was pronounced. When finished, the gare-ridge would house the black Buick, which for the time being stood under a roof attached to the house itself. Aunt Edith referred to this roof as the "porte cochère."

Best of all, in the back yard sat a playhouse with a porch and real windows with white lace curtains. It had a red, blue, and yellow braided rug, and a staircase that led up to a second storey tall enough for dolls to stand in. Two ladies lived next door, their big house half hidden by enormous lilacs, mock orange and locust trees. On the opposite side of Uncle Pent's, a board fence concealed the small house where "Uncle" John and "Aunt" Ella lived. They were the children of the slaves of the former owners of Uncle Pent's property. Their former owners had given them the house and its small plot of land. Their son Washington wriggled through an open gate in the fence, to play with my cousin Lil, who was his age.

As a country child, I was an early riser. Hours before the house awoke, I listened to the rattle of wheels and clop of hooves in the street. At each new sound, I ran to the window. In the early light I saw the milkman arrive, then the iceman bringing ice for Aunt Edith's two big iceboxes. I crept downstairs, and out to the porte cochère. I climbed onto the Buick's cool black leather seat, which was exactly like the seats in our best buggy at home.

Aunt Edith played the piano, and so did each of my five cousins. To my ear, the sound of the piano was thin and tinny compared to the rich chords of Mama's little reed organ. On the piano's music rack were propped books called "Études," which I took to be the name of the composer.

One afternoon Uncle Pent, dressed in a long crisply ironed tan linen coat and a tan cap and goggles, invited Papa and me to come for a ride in the Buick. My cousins came too, except for Jane, who at seventeen considered herself above going on jaunts with children. She condescended, however, to lend me her veil and duster. Ann, Nell and I sat on the automobile's smooth back seat, with Lil on a folding bench at our feet. Addie sat up front between Papa and Uncle Pent.

Papa cranked the engine. A number of small boys materialized, as if from nowhere, to watch. Among them was Washington from next door. The neighbor ladies from the tall house came out onto their porch, and other ladies appeared in doorways, down the street. When at last we got going, the little boys trotted alongside for as far as they could keep up, staring intently into our faces. At an intersection, a man driving a wagon pulled over, jumped down, and held his horse's head to let us pass. At another intersection, Uncle Pent pulled over to let a team of horses go ahead of us.

I began to find the automobile's throbbing motion unpleasant. Ann pressed a peppermint into my hand. "Close your eyes" she advised.

Uncle Pent announced important sights. I opened my eyes. "Here's the courthouse, Nellie," he said. "Here's Everett House. It's made of logs, like home. Stonewall Jackson had his headquarters here. And this is the Federal

Building. That window on the left, on the second floor, is where your Papa works."

Abruptly he turned to Papa. "Jack, I think Nellie's had enough." With much backing and filling, he turned the automobile around and we headed back the way we had come. The same crowd of little boys watched us arrive. Then the unpleasant jolting stopped, and I felt better.

Uncle Pent told me that the idea of having an automobile was Aunt Edith's. He preferred his buggy. "Nellie," he asked me one day, "would you like to come with Moll and me?" Moll was his gentle old bay mare.

He tucked a tan buggy robe over our knees. "We don't want to get our shoes dusty," he said. Soon we were rolling along luxuriously on the buggy's modern rubber-tired wheels, at Moll's sedate pace.

From time to time Uncle Pent flicked his reins and said mildly, "Oh come on, Moll, you can do better than that." Moll broke into a trot, but a moment later, she dropped back to her unhurried walk. Uncle Pent smelled like cigars. Much as I admired him, I wondered what Mama would say about his smoking.

We arrived in a narrow back street. Colored children gathered around. My uncle carried his big satchel into one small house, then another. The children kept a respectful distance from the buggy but stared somberly up at me. I stared somberly back.

Uncle Pent told me, as we set off for home, "Your aunt wants me to give up Moll and drive the automobile, Nellie. She wants me to stop coming to this part of town. But I can't do that, now, can I?"

"No, sir," I said.

It was dark when we arrived back at Uncle Pent's. Aunt Edith met us on the porch.

"Up to that 'neighborhood' again?" she asked his forehead.

"Yep," he replied, with practiced nonchalance.

"You can't be seen in that neighborhood, Pent. Think of what it's doing to your daughters' reputations."

DEATH

When Grandpa Wister died, in November, 1902, I was seven. I remember Grandpa's body lying on a cot in a corner of the big downstairs front room that had been his and Grandma's bedroom. I heard, "When the coffin comes we'll put him in it." Then Grandma Cody appeared, smelling of Pears soap and her horse, Jenny. "You boys are coming home with me," she said. Dayton was six, Hugh was four. Our one-year-old sister, Bess, stayed with Mama.

I may have missed Grandpa a little. I may have missed hearing his dragging steps and the hesitating thump of his cane. I was too young for his death to make much of an impression.

Two years later, when Grandma died, it was spring and school was out. She'd had asthma all her life, and in her last years, a heart condition. One morning Mama, very upset, sent me to get Mrs. Flood. Mama said, "Quick, Nellie! Fast as you can! Don't stop for anything!"

Mrs. Flood lived close by. I had been sent to get her before. The last time was when our sister was born. I hurried to Floods'. My friend Maud was at the gate.

"Come look at my playhouse, Nellie," Maud said, "Ma gave me a piece of carpet to put in it."

Maud's playhouse was a space under the kitchen steps. I followed her up the lane to the kitchen porch. Together we squatted by an opening in the lattice, then crawled in. There, in the gloom, a piece of carpet covered the trampled dirt.

Over our heads, footsteps came and went. Mrs. Flood and her sister, Aunt Betty Ann, were getting dinner. Soon, someone crossed the porch and thumped down the steps. Floods' dinner bell rang, then right away, up the valley, ours echoed it.

In a panic, I backed out of the playhouse and hurried up the steps.

In the kitchen Mrs. Flood said, "Why, child, what in the world...?" She was already reaching for her bonnet.

By the time we got home, Mama was sitting by the window in Grandma's room. Mrs. Neff, from the farm below Floods', was bending over Grandma.

"Go on out, child, and play," Mrs. Neff said in a kindly voice that told me we had come too late.

For years afterward, I refused to go near Maud's playhouse. Even the sight of those kitchen steps brought back the painful memory of the morning when, because of me, Mama had waited alone.

* * *

Grandma's body lay on the same cot in the same room as Grandpa's had, two years before. I lay on Grandma's bed, on the edge of the quilt. I could just see Grandma's ruffled cap, her small profile, between the sleeves of my uncles' coats. They had come by stage and train from Martinsburg and Baltimore to sit up with the body until Baxter Flood, who was in the hauling business, arrived with the coffin. Why Mr. Priest, way over in Minerva, had to make Grandma's coffin, I don't know. Perhaps Mr. Waybright, who generally made the coffins in Chinkapin Creek, was busy.

I thought Grandma looked asleep. Then, on the bed where she herself had slept not long before, I too fell asleep.

I was abruptly startled awake. I was not alone on the bed. Carefully I turned my head and saw Maud's big brother, Baxter Flood.

I was deeply shocked. Baxter had driven eleven miles to Minerva, then had had to wait for the coffin to be finished, before bringing it back with him. One of the ladies had said, "Go lie on the bed by Nellie, Bax, see if you can get some sleep." Still, to lie on a bed with a young man, even on top of the quilt, was scandalous. Other people were in the room, neighbor ladies, including Baxter's own stepmother. I carefully slithered off of the bed and found my way to a chair, hoping nobody had noticed.

Those two powerful memories stay with me: one, of having failed Mama when she needed me most; and the other, of lying on the same bed with a young man of sixteen.

However unreasonably, I still have the conviction that, if not for me, Grandma would have still been sitting there, her sweet rosy face smiling as it always had. She'd still have been talking to us in her lovely North of Ireland accent, and smoking her evening pipe of Shiffman's Asthma Remedy.

The Southern Methodist minister delivered his eulogy from the hallway, so that he could be heard in the bedroom and the parlor. When he said, "Amen," Papa's brothers, raised by Grandma to be Methodists, said, "Amen," with him. This was an unsettling thing for a little Presbyterian girl to hear. As I was taught, a congregation should be quiet.

Grandma's coffin sat on two chairs facing each other. She no longer looked merely asleep. In the harsh morning light, she looked old and thin, so shrunken she no longer resembled anyone I had ever known.

In the parlor Mama whispered, "Nellie. Dayton. I want to talk to you."

Dayton and I left the coffin and followed Mama down the hall, into the dining room. She closed the door behind us.

"The only part of a person that dies is the body," Mama said. "What your saw in there isn't Grandma. That's her body. Her soul is in heaven. Remember that. Grandma is with everyone she loved. They were waiting for her to join them, and now she has."

Neighbor men dug the grave, carried the coffin out to the spring wagon, then drove it to Papa's family's graveyard, on the knoll above our springhouse.

That fall, in the schoolhouse yard at recess, Maud Flood said, "Let's walk up the hill and see Miz Fanny Hunter's baby girl."

The Hunters' baby had died. On the doctor's open front door hung a black ribbon. We heard hushed voices, inside. In the parlor stood a low table with a tiny, open coffin. Wearing a long lace-trimmed dress, a baby lay there, with a wizened oldman's face, as if made of clay. It hardly seemed that it could ever have been alive.

Women were in the parlor. One said, "There's another little angel." I thought of Mama's words to Dayton and me. What Maud and I saw was only the baby's body. Its soul had gone to heaven, and perhaps at that moment Grandma was rocking it to sleep, as she used to rock me.

Modern Plumbing

Every Saturday night, Papa built up a hot fire under the water reservoir of the kitchen stove. He carried in a big tin bathtub and set it on the kitchen floor. He then strung towels around the tub, for privacy. He carried the heated water in a kettle from the stove. Papa got the first bath, then came Mama. We children generally had quite a wait, and by then the water was pretty cool. Afterward, my brothers dragged the tepid brown water out to the garden, or dumped it into the swill tub for the hogs.

None of Papa's brothers' families had to endure this ordeal: they all had bathrooms. In Martinsburg, Uncle Pent's bathtub was a luxurious ornate affair, made of copper and long enough for a tall man to lie flat. It occupied its own permanent spot. Two spigots delivered hot and cold water directly into the tub, and a hole in the bottom carried the wastewater out.

In Uncle Pent's bathroom there was, besides the bathtub, a pedestal sink with pink moss roses painted inside the china basin, with two spigots, for hot and cold water. He had something else as well: a "water closet," where you could relieve yourself, without going outdoors to the backhouse, or privy, as we did on our farm.

When Grandpa Wister ran our farm, he laid down V-shaped wooden conduits from the natural spring on the mountainside, across our pasture-fields to the house, the henhouse, the washhouse, and the milk house. Conduits also went to the log troughs at the barns, the calf lot, the front lot where we watered our horses, and to a metal sink outside our kitchen porch. That's where where our hired women drew water for cooking, and filled the big pitchers we used for washing in our bedrooms. In the wintertime, we often had to break skims of ice that formed on the tops of these pitchers.

"Everybody in town has a bathroom, Carrie." Papa said one day to Mama. "Don't you think we ought to put one in?"

He'd made up his mind before he spoke. Mama knew this, so she said yes.

Papa hired Mr. Fred Tolley to make the renovations. Mr. Fred was a burly, slow-moving man with a nervous habit: whenever anything troubled him, he cleared his throat. Though a skilled carpenter, Mr. Fred had never seen a bathroom. When Papa showed him the designs, he eyed them suspiciously, and cleared his throat.

I had traveled with Papa and used Uncle Pent's bathroom. Therefore I appointed myself our resident expert on such things. "Oh yes," I told my schoolmates, "It's a room *inside* the house. You don't have to heat water in the kitchen. You don't have to carry water or dump it afterward."

Our teacher took me aside one day, and handed me a package. That evening, I helped Mama unwrap a linen panel. Hemmed, embroidered and framed by Miss Annie herself, it was to hang over our new bathtub. In gleaming crimson floss she had stitched this message: "COME IN AND SPLASH."

Two of our hired men dug trenches to lay metal pipes to replace Grandpa's old wooden conduits. To the sounds of Mr. Fred's saw and chisel, a new doorway was cut in the upstairs hallway, over the kitchen.

Underneath the new bathroom, Mr. Fred made space for a water heater. He also left a space for pipes for a future kitchen sink. Every time he took up his saw or chisel, he cleared his throat.

I remember the day a team of draft horses appeared in our lot, pulling a road-wagon that sagged under the weight of four enormous crates. Inside one crate was a white-enameled cast iron bathtub equipped with what the manufacturer called "French feet," (plain knobs, I seem to remember). Inside a second crate were piping and accessories. In the last two crates were a sink like Uncle Pent's, but without the painted flowers, and a water closet. Before Mr. Fred unpacked the last item, he suggested Mama and our hired girls go indoors; water closets were not to be unpacked in mixed company.

Our hired woman, Mrs. Pennybacker, came to Mama with a question: "Mrs. Wister, shall I gather up the wash sets and chambers and carry them up to the attic?" She referred to the pitchers, washbowls, and chamber pots, which were kept in the bedrooms. They had to be emptied, washed, and refilled every day: it took a great deal of work to maintain them.

"Don't put them away yet," Mama said.

Near the end of Mr. Fred's big job installing our modern plumbing, he stopped clearing his throat.

Over the new bathtub, Mama hung Miss Annie's panel with its cheery invitation to "COME IN AND SPLASH."

One morning, soon after all this, I happened to be in the kitchen when suddenly I heard a great crashing noise as if cows were stampeding through a river, directly overhead. At the top of the back stairs, as I hurried up to investigate, I saw a wave of water shoot out from under the new bathroom door.

Inside the room, rigid with shock and disapproval, stood my five-year-old-sister Elsie. In the bathtub, naked, squatted her friend, Lettie Morgan. "Come in and splash!" she shrieked. "Come in and splash!" She spanked the surface of the water with both hands. A fresh sheet of water sailed across the tub's rim.

"You read very well, Lettie," Mama said, quite calmly. "Now suppose we get you out of there," she said in the softest of voices. "Then we will clean up this mess."

* * *

In time, Mama and our hired girls put away forever the big china water pitchers and wash bowls that had adorned our bedrooms with their beautiful hand-painted bouquets of rambler roses and bleeding hearts and ragged robins. The chamber pots, however, went on being useful, as did our old privy. A single bathroom, in a big busy house like ours, turned out to be scarcely adequate, after all.

Years later, after Mama's death, I, then a woman of about sixty, sorted through the contents of the old press that stood just outside the bathroom door. Under a pile of sheets Mama had set aside to be mended, I discovered Miss Annie's embroidery. The cloth had turned yellow, its beautiful crimson floss had faded to a dull brown. Yet, the cheery message brought back the sprightly image of Lettie slapping the water with both hands as she crowed, "Come in and splash! Come in and splash!"

* * *

The worst thing that ever happened in our new bathroom involved a man named Jake who used to help us out in corn-cutting season.

Papa hired him because he was a dependable, hard worker. He was a terrible know-it-all, and very unpopular with the other men. The year we put in our bathroom, Jake made a point of announcing in his loud, superior voice, "I hear you-all finally put in a bathroom." The impression he gave was that it was high time we'd gotten around to this improvement. He himself lived in a desolate little hollow, twelve miles from our farm, where I doubt there are many bathrooms even today.

All the same, one of our hired men took Jake aside. "When you want to get water to wash, you turn on a gadget that's in a bowl," he said. "And after you use the water closet, you pull a chain that's up on the wall. That'll clean it out."

"I know all that," Jake said, in his cocky, off-hand way.

If Jake had to get up in the night, he'd go outside, as did all the other men who worked for us, even after we got the bathroom. Surely Jake, who'd been with us for a month, that year, would make a point of inspecting the bathroom, with nobody around to observe him doing it. He might brag about how well he knew bathrooms, but he wouldn't be likely to try it for himself.

What made Jake decide to use the new bathroom, without at least an inspection in daylight, no one will ever know. At the last moment, I'm sure he regretted having been so offhand with Reuben. He must have been in a fearsome hurry.

There was a place, he knew, with a chain, but when he went to look for the chain it was too late: he had used the wrong contraption. Not only was there no chain, but the thing itself had been inconveniently high and hard to sit on. In the dark, he crept back to the hired men's room, dragged on his overalls, fumbled out his cap, his extra shirts and bandanna handkerchief, and left, never to return.

I'm sure Papa missed Jake. It's even possible our other men did as well. He had come to us for years, and had done his share of hard work. But Mama, our hired girls, and my little sisters weren't sorry at all. I especially wasn't. I was the one who had to help clean up the mess.

Nellie Wister with turkeys

ANDREW WAYBRIGHT

Waybrights were considered "strange" in our community. Really, they weren't so different. Mr. Waybright was a carpenter who, among his many projects, built coffins. Some people just could not get past that. They came from the Shenandoah Valley of Virginia, only about 30 miles across the border. In those days, 30 miles was as good as a thousand. It was not only their "Valley" customs, but their own family ways, as well, that put them at odds with some.

In 1908, my end-of-school exercises were held in the evening. Since Mama didn't approve of children being out alone after dark, she sent our young hired girl, Ola Smith, to keep me company. I wore long black worsted stockings and heavy high-topped shoes. My hair was in pigtails, each one looped to stand up above my ears. I was thirteen. During the exercises, a full moon rose.

As I came out of the schoolhouse, a voice said, "May I walk you home?" It was Andrew Waybright. I had suspected that he admired me, but I never gave him a second thought.

For the first time, I looked closely at Andrew. He was handsome. At that moment, I couldn't recall a single strange thing he had ever done.

Ola gave me a disapproving frown. "What will your Pa say about you walking home with a Waybright?" she said.

I looked back at Andrew. His whole world seemed to hang upon my answer. I told Ola to go on ahead. She took off up the road at a brisk pace. I knew she would tattle on me.

Andrew and I set off up the hill. Ahead of us, Mr. Neffs' tin roof reflected the cornmeal color of the newly risen moon. At Uncle Pent's former property, the boxwoods cast dense black shadows. Dust, fine as talc, rose around our feet. A whippoorwill called. A small waterway sparkled in the moonlight alongside the road.

"I dare you to wade in that," I said. The little stream was famous for its icy water. I bent down and unlaced my shoes, took them off, and dropped my stockings into them.

Andrew followed suit, and we splashed into the frigid stream. Instantly my feet went numb, and I scrambled out. He did the same, then picked up both our shoes by their laces and slung them over his shoulder. Barefoot, we set off again. He was a slender, serious boy with brown hair, tall for his age.

The road's warm soft dust felt wonderfully comforting. I thought how nice it was to walk home with a boy who carried my shoes.

"What are you going to be when you grow up?" He asked me.

"I want to be a nurse," I said, "but Papa will never let me. He thinks nursing is menial."

"Nothing is menial unless *you* think it is," Andrew said. "You can be anything you want to be."

An owl skimmed silently along our orchard fence. Andrew was so tall, I had to tilt my head back to look up into his eyes. How sure of himself he sounded!

"I'm going to be an astronomer," he said. "Charlottesville has an observatory." He peered down into my face. "You have pretty eyes, Nellie."

I blushed. I had spent long moments in front of Mama's looking glass, wishing my dark straight brows were arched and fine. "My brother teases me about my pigtails," I said. "He says they make me look like a bull calf with horns."

"Your brother's wrong," Andrew said. "You're like a redwing blackbird: no one can tell how pretty a redwing is until it flies. You're almost ready to fly."

We reached our gate. I heard the creaking sound of Mama's rocking chair. She was waiting by the open window. The ploughshare weight on our gate clanged behind Andrew and me.

"Thank you for walking me home," I whispered, too green to know the customary thing was for *him* to thank *me*.

"Would you mind if I called on you again?" he asked.

"I'd like that very much," I answered.

* * *

"Walking home with a Waybright!" scoffed Dayton the next morning.

"That's right. What of it?" I asked.

"Waybrights are strange! His Papa builds coffins!"

"What's wrong with building coffins?" I demanded.

"It's only the worst luck in the whole wide world!" blurted Ola, our superstitious hired girl. "You're just asking for some kind of spell to come down on this house! Heaven protect us."

"Oh Ola, enlightened people don't believe in those things any more," I scolded.

Ola indignantly snatched the empty biscuit plate and stormed off to the kitchen.

"Once and for all, there's nothing strange about Andrew Waybright," I told Dayton.

"How about the way his old man talked to Papa before the election?" Dayton countered. "Said he wouldn't vote for him, even though Papa lent him all that money to send his boy to medical school. You don't think that's strange?"

"I credit a man for speaking his mind," Papa interrupted us. "Honesty's a rare quality."

* * *

"I saw you walking home with Andrew Waybright," Maud Flood said during lunch at school the next day.

"They're strange." Maud motioned toward the Waybright children. "Look at them over there, eating that big fancy pie off of those fancy plates. Bone-handled knives and forks, linen napkins! Why don't they just grab a chunk, like the rest of the boys?"

"Good manners make you strange?" I asked.

"Who do they think they are? Their dad makes coffins!"

I turned my back on Maud.

* * *

One morning, the ploughshare weight on our gate clanged, and I saw Andrew making his way up our lawn. Flustered, I made my hair presentable, then went to the door.

He wore overalls, and his hair was tousled. He carried a bucket.

"My ma heard that your ma loves Jersey milk. Since we're the only ones with a Jersey cow, she thought she'd send you some."

I guided him out onto the porch and closed the door. "Andrew, I was looking forward to seeing you again." I knew, however, that a girl shouldn't appear overly eager.

Mama appeared from the kitchen, drying a dish. Seeing Andrew, her face brightened. "Why Andrew, how nice to see you," she said.

That night I lay awake thinking about the red-winged blackbird which hides its gold and scarlet markings until it takes wing. Its liquid gurgle was the very sound of spring. The day's heat drained from the old house. The worn joists and floorboards creaked. Moonlight reflected in the wash-bowl beside my bed. A redwing!... A nurse!...

* * *

"Andrew Waybright's come down with something," Maud Flood announced the next day. "Typhoid fever, they think. His folks have sent for Luke. Now ain't that typical Waybright to send for their son, when Dr. Sam Hunter here is good enough for the rest of us... and could come quicker!"

I wondered if wading in the icy creek had made Andrew sick. I worried that Luke wouldn't come in time.

An old book on home medicine occupied a shelf in Mama's room. Its red cloth cover was faded, its pages softened with age. It had belonged to Grandma Wister. Pure air in a sickroom is vital, it advised. Air could be purified by steeping rosin in hot water. Poultices could be made of willow bark, slippery elm or oatmeal; also of yeast or linseed meal or bread or charcoal. I searched the old book for some remedy for typhoid fever. It said that brewed water gruel, mutton tea, and calf's foot jelly could benefit typhoid sufferers. I imagined myself wearing a starched white apron and nurse's cap, steeping cloths in vinegar, and placing them on Andrew's forehead.

Maud appeared that evening, and said that Dr. Luke Waybright had not yet arrived. I resolved that the next morning I would take Grandma's book to Waybrights', and nurse Andrew myself.

The next day, Maud told us Andrew had died. Seeing my stricken face, she didn't tease me. In fact, everybody tiptoed around me. Even Dayton gave up his chair for me when there was no other place to sit. "Told you making coffins was bad luck," Ola whispered. Mama told her to "keep quiet."

Since typhoid fever is contagious, Waybrights held no wake. They buried Andrew in the small graveyard on their property. The Arbaughs, who had first settled there, had marked their graves with plain stone slabs. For Andrew, his family erected a tall, white marble obelisk that could be seen for miles. "They sent all the way to Harrisonburg for that stone," Maud said. "Just like Waybrights: always putting on airs."

"Hush, Maud," Mama said. "The boy is dead."

One day Mama said, "Nellie, your Papa and I drove past Waybrights'. I never saw anything as beautiful as the vine on their porch."

"I'll ask Mrs. Waybright for a cutting, Mama," I said. I wanted to see where Andrew had lived. I drove our buggy. Andrew's mother appeared on the porch. She was tall, as

Andrew had been. She laid a hand on the buggy's whip socket.

"Andrew was so happy to have walked home with you that night," she said, and her voice broke. She invited me in.

I don't know what I expected to find inside Waybrights' house. It was surprisingly similar to ours. There were the same Brussels carpet and homemade rag carpeting, the same odors of ripening apples and lye soap. They had the same magazines and newspapers: The *Ladies' Home Journal*, *The Delineator*, *House and Garden*, *Country Gentleman*, *The Baltimore Sun*, and The *Guthrie County Review*.

Andrew's mother opened the door to a small space off the kitchen. "We moved him down here when he got so sick," she said. "I wanted to look after him myself."

In the small pantry, jars of canned peaches and apple butter crowded the overhead shelves. Mrs. Waybright passed her hand along the wall of the little room. "His bed was here," she said.

I gazed at the empty space and imagined him there, his handsome face drawn in pain.

Outside on the porch, Mrs. Waybright produced a spade and a quantity of damp newspaper. Together we severed a length of the big wisteria, then wrapped its cut end in the paper. "He'll be glad you have a piece of this," she said, glancing up the hill at the marble monument. Leaning across the bundle, she kissed me.

People didn't kiss each other in those days, at least in our part of West Virginia, they didn't. Rattled, I failed to hear what she said next. But as I drove home, her words came to me. "He had my dad's eyes. As long as he lived, it was like having Dad back. Now they're both gone."

* * *

Mrs. Waybright's wisteria shoot bloomed the fifth year after Mama and I planted it. You might expect the first bloom to be sparse but, as Mama said, it was "Just like a purple curtain."

"What's that vine on your fence, Carrie?" Mrs. Flood asked.

"Wisteria. Mrs. Waybright gave it to us," Mama said.

"Waybrights!" Mrs. Flood said disparagingly. "It's going to take over that nice goose-plum tree Jack's dad planted. You ought to pull it down."

* * *

Papa served on the Board of Regents for West Virginia's preparatory schools. "Nursing's not for you, Nellie," he told me with a finality that quenched my hopes. He chose a boarding school in Lewisburg, which did not offer nursing.

When I came down with appendicitis, Papa brought me home to recuperate. One afternoon, he approached me in the garden. Holding two letters addressed to him, he said, "One of these is from Marshall College. Were you thinking of going there?"

"They have a nursing program, Papa," I held my breath...

He stuffed the Marshall letter into his pocket and held up the other letter. "This one's from your school in Lewisburg."

Deep lines had developed on either side of his mouth. He wore reading glasses. For the first time I realized that he was growing old.

He opened the second letter. "Your alumnae office offers you a job in a new district high school in Monroe County," he said. "I know the trustees. They must think highly of you."

Sweat-bees swarmed under my broad-brimmed hat. What would please Papa most, I knew, would be for me to take the job in Monroe County.

* * *

My Monroe County students were earnest young women and big, loose-limbed boys, barely younger than I. My subject, advertised as home economics, turned out to be algebra and Latin. I came home just as our wisteria bloomed. Mama asked me to take a branch of it to Mrs. Waybright."

"Take some locust too," she said. Locusts were her favorite blossom.

Long before I arrived at Andrew's house I could see his monument. I thought what an unusual ambition Andrew had had to study astronomy. The lemony scent of locust blossoms and the odd sweetness of wisteria filled the air.

Waybrights' house had the look some places get after the children have grown and gone. Mrs. Waybright appeared in the doorway. Her hair had turned gray. Mr. Waybright materialized in the door of the carpentry shop. His hair too was gray.

I lifted my bouquet from the front seat, meaning to say, "Here are some flowers from Mama," I said, instead, "Here are some flowers for Andrew."

A paling fence separated Andrew's grave from the old Arbaugh plot. I carried my bouquet up to the base of

Andrew's monument. His grave was deeply sunken. If he had lived, I thought, he might have become an astronomer. I might have become a nurse. Might I have married him? I felt a tightness in my chest. As I drove the automobile out of the lane, I was followed by Mr. and Mrs. Waybright's gaze, reflected in my rear-view mirror.

* * *

Andrew's older brother, Hinshaw, paid me a surprise visit at the public school were I taught in Monroe County. When I returned home for a short time, he called on me. He was twenty-nine and hadn't married. I was twenty-six, and single as well. On our porch, Mama's plant stand, painted green, was filled with fragrant red and white petunias. Letters on the fresh red paint of our newest barn read, "JACK WISTER & SONS, LIVESTOCK." Hinshaw wore a lightweight, fancy-weave tan suit and carried a flat-brimmed straw hat. I said, "I guess salesmen get more money than preachers, Hinshaw."

He had once wanted to be a preacher.

He flushed. Rotating his hat in his sunburned hands, he said slowly, "I came to ask you to marry me."

I was astonished!

"Hinshaw," I said, "You'll make a fine husband for some woman some day, but we hardly know each other. What put such an idea into your head?"

Seeing the hurt in his eyes, I felt bad. He said, "Andrew was always my folks' favorite. They wanted to see you and him married. I guess I thought if you and I... sounds foolish when I say it out loud..."

He rose and made his way down the lawn, leaving the gate open.

Mama appeared at the screen door. "Did I hear right? Did Hinshaw Waybright just ask you to marry him?"

"He did, Mama," I replied.

"You said 'no,' of course."

"Of course I said no. But I felt terrible, Mama. I still do."

"It's all right, Nellie. That family is going through a lot right now." A wry smile came to her face. "And he's left the gate open."

Years later, I married, moved away, and had children. One day I returned to visit. As I walked back to the farm from the village, sunlight glinted off the surface of the spring where Andrew and I had waded so long ago. I hadn't thought about the little waterway in years. Curiosity drew me down through a dense thicket. Time had changed the irrepressible meanderings of the little stream.

Typhoid fever is caused by a germ, not by getting one's feet cold; still, I couldn't help feeling responsible for Andrew's death. Could I have saved him by pleading with him not to give up? If he had lived, might I have become a nurse? We might have married and I might have had his children. But those things were not to be. Like a small country stream, life goes where it will.

EM CLAYTON

Em Clayton worked for us from around 1895 until 1910. Squat and red-faced, she was as stubborn as an old laying hen. On washday mornings, she came plodding up our farm lane while it was still dark. She filled her iron kettle, set it on top the old kettle stove in our washhouse, and got a good fire going under it. While her water came to a boil, she crossed the yard to the house and joined us for breakfast.

Em wasn't young, and we had a lot for her to do. She washed all of Papa's shirts and nightshirts and BVDs, all of Mama's wash dresses and underwear, all the dresses and underclothes of my little sisters and me, and my brothers' pants and shirts and underclothes. She washed clothing that belonged to the hired men and women who lived in our house, and linens from a dozen beds. Mama often glanced out across the yard to see Em, bent over her work inside the open doorway of the wash house, or with her mouth full of clothespins as she pegged the clean laundry on the clotheslines. Each time, she said, "I do wish we had one of those new washing machines for Em."

One day Mama handed Papa a copy of *Woman's Home Companion,* opened to a picture of a modern barrel-shaped wooden washing machine set on legs and equipped with a hand crank. "I wish you'd show this to Ed, Jack," she said.

Mr. Ed Sanderson owned a mercantile business in Minerva, our county seat. Papa showed him Mama's magazine. Mr. Ed promised to travel to Baltimore and find us the very best and most up-to-date washing machine there was.

"Hotel size, Ed," Papa reminded him, "we have a big family and lots of visitors."

"By the way, Jack, you might be interested in this," Mr. Ed said, and he showed Papa a picture of a water heater. "I just got one of these for Molly."

"While I was about it, Carrie," Papa said when he came home, "I ordered a hot water tank."

The only way we could heat water in the kitchen was by hand-filling the reservoir in the big range, then building a fire in the range's firebox to bring the water to a boil. Mama said she would be pleased to have a hot water tank.

Papa also ordered a new kitchen sink.

Not long afterward, a heavy road wagon came creaking up our farm lane and across the lot, drawn by two powerful work horses. Strapped on the back of the wagon were three wooden crates. Our hired men helped unpacked them.

Mr. Fred Tolley, Papa's friend who knew about these things, set the heater in the kitchen next to the range where Mama wanted it. He connected its pipes to the new sink. He was just finishing the work when Em Clayton sidled in the open doorway.

Mr. Fred looked around. "What's the matter, Em?" he asked.

"You remember that-there threshing machine that blew up down at the creek, that time when all them men got scalded?"

Mr. Fred remembered the accident. A steam boiler on a threshing machine had exploded and badly injured the members of a threshing crew. But there was a difference, he told Em, between steam boilers on threshing machines and water heaters inside houses. He told her there would be no steam under pressure in our water tank.

Em listened. Unconvinced, she awkwardly turned and trudged back to the washhouse.

The following week, she stood in the kitchen doorway, as tense as a dog catching the scent of a wildcat, staring at the water tank. Em edged gingerly around the farthest side of the table, to her seat. I doubt she tasted any of her breakfast that day.

Later, if you happened to cross the yard in front of the open washhouse, you'd see Em inside. She dipped up home-made soft lye soap with a gourd and rubbed it into whatever items lay on the washboard, all as usual, but with a new, worried frown on her face.

I was only a little girl, but I looked down on Em because she wasn't married, so her children had no legal father. One of her offspring, a boy younger than me, sometimes hung around our farm, because he lived with Em's parents who were our tenants.

Our new washing machine looked like a barrel that had been sawed in half and set on legs. It had a hand crank on one side and, on the other, hoses that connected it to a spigot and a drain. It was, Papa told us, the best money could buy; it had been designed for "hotels and boarding houses; it was "guaranteed," he said, "to wash five shirts at one time without using a washboard;" and "a child could operate it without fatigue." Now, he said, Em wouldn't have to carry water to fill a kettle, or scrub so hard.

"Isn't that nice, Em," Mama said. "You won't even need a washboard. All you have to do is turn the crank."

Frowning, Em eyed the intruder, her fat work-red-dened hands clenched at her sides. She waited until Mama had gone back to the house. Then she set up her ancient kettle, as she always had, and got down the familiar old washboard. When she had finished for the day and was on her way home, she stopped to tell her brother, Pee Clayton, who worked for us, "I don't come walkin' all the way down here before sun-up to crank no churn."

Mama found this funny, but Papa wasn't amused. "Does she have any idea what all that cost, with the rail freight and hauling charges from the depot?" he said. "Does she know we put it in just for her?"

"I doubt it," Mama said.

"I really think she'd like to go back to the old days and wash down in the run in the calf lot," Papa said, referring to the icy spring runoff where women had washed their clothes for generations.

The next time Mama saw Em, she said, "Mr. Wister went to so much trouble to make your work easier, Em, you really should at least try to use the new machine."

Em stuck out her lower lip. "Mrs. Wister," she said, "I can't get men's shirts clean without work."

As Em neared sixty, younger women came to help her use our new machines, but she stuck to her old methods. Every time she appeared in the kitchen doorway, she gave the "boiler," as she called the hot water tank, a worried look. she muttered, to no one in particular, "I cain't git men's shirts clean without work."

She said this every time without fail, and always with a satisfied expression on her sullen red face.

JONAH SMITH

Jonah Smith was the only hired man we ever had whom Mama invited into the sitting room in the evening when Papa wasn't home. Mama liked Jonah because he could sing. She learned this when, soon after he came to work for us, she noticed a tuning fork in his shirt pocket.

"Jonah, do you play a instrument?" she asked.

He turned crimson and looked quickly away. "I play the banjo," he muttered. Mama, sensing something more, waited. He whispered, "And I sing."

Jonah was so bashful that whenever Mama came into a room, he'd leave. He wouldn't even look at a little girl like me. If he was in the kitchen when I came in, he'd turn away and the back of his bald head would turn bright red. If people he didn't know were at our table, he'd leave the food on his plate and go off somewhere, his face as red as his bandanna. His head would turn such a painful dark red that everyone else suffered too. What little blond hair he had left had grey in it, as if something had happened to age him prematurely. He was only twenty.

I never saw any other men as bashful as Jonah, except two brothers, Arthur and Albert Mitchell, from Mount Zion. They also worked for us. When the Mitchell brothers were in the kitchen with Jonah, the three of them sat, silent as owls.

Little by little, Jonah got used to us. One evening, Mama came out to the kitchen after supper. She found him sitting alone, softly playing his banjo, singing under his breath.

Besides Jonah's bashfulness, he had his own way of walking, which was a long-legged swinging lope, as he bent a little forward from the hips. You could always pick out Jonah among the other men in the fields, a quarter of a mile away.

After Jonah began to feel at home with us, he came into the kitchen and read his Bible. He read without a break, never looking up. He read everything else the same way, be it the newspapers piled on the kitchen windowsill, or Mama's magazines, *The Christian Observer* and *The Christian Endeavor.* Jonah read every one of them, without a pause and without looking up, just going from page one right through to the end.

Mama liked Jonah's quiet manner, and the fact that while the other men went off to the barn to chew tobacco, he read. One winter night, when Mama and he were the only ones in the kitchen, she asked, "Would you like to come in the sitting room and sing a hymn with us before bedtime, Jonah? With Mr. Wister not here the children and I sound a little thin."

Jonah blushed painfully and didn't answer. Presently we heard a knock at the sitting room door, and there he stood. That night, for the first time, we got the full range of his voice. Singing to himself, he had held it in so as not to disturb the rest of the household, but in the sitting room, with Mama's permission, he let it out in a pure, true, strong tenor. "Blest Be the Tie that Binds," he sang with us. Our small childrens' voices, reedy and immature, and Mama's sweet, rather weak soprano sounded wonderful in harmony with Jonah. As he sang he looked at each one of us, one after the other, straight in the eye, in a confident, easy way, as he would never have dared before. His blue eyes looked dreamy and filled with pleasure.

We grew to love the evenings when, after supper, Mama would say, "Jonah, will you come in the sitting room to hear the lesson and sing with us?"

We sang one favorite hymn after the other; "Bringing in the Sheaves," "Let the Lower Lights Be Burning," and "Now the Day is Over."

Jonah hadn't far to go to spend Sundays with his family, which was just down the road at Uncle Ike Cody's, where his parents lived in Uncle Ike's tenant house. He went there every Sunday, after helping to milk and feed our animals. One day he came back from Uncle Ike's and went straight to Mama. He stood in front of her, twisting his hat in his fingers.

"What is it, Jonah?" Mama asked.

Blushing, Jonah said, "I aim to git married."

"Is it someone we know, Jonah?"

"Sadie Mitchell."

"That wouldn't be Arthur and Albert's sister?"

Jonah nodded. Mama thought that would be an interesting match. She said, "Bring your Sadie here, Jonah. Mr. Wister's planning to build a tenant house at the mountain."

Mr. Fred Tolley, who did all our carpentering, built the house with Jonah's help. They built it above our spring-house run, on a bench of land that had the mountain at its back and a view out over the valley. Huckleberry bushes grew there, and there was a place for a garden, if Sadie wanted it. It had five rooms.

To furnish Jonah's house, Mama sent up chairs and tables from the milk house loft. She sent a bed that had been stored for years, and a cupboard Mr. Fred had taken out of our kitchen when he altered it. All these things were handmade and very old. Some of them had belonged to Mama's family, and some to Papa's.

Jonah married Sadie. We heard the story about the wedding and afterward. The guests drove from Mount Zion to Uncle Ike's for the "infare" which was the dinner that bridegrooms' families always gave newly married couples. When the time came for the guests to sit down, no one could find Jonah.

Albert and Arthur looked in the barn and in the milk house. They looked in the hen house and the garden and along the river. Then someone thought of the pigpen. There they found Jonah in his good blue suit, carrying a bucket of slops for the hogs.

"Come on in the house, Jonah," Arthur said. "Everybody's waiting on you."

"You-all go right on and eat," Jonah said. "I have to slop the hogs."

In my family, after this, when any one of us didn't want to do something or couldn't come when called, we said, "You-all go right on and eat, I have to slop the hogs."

Sadie turned out to be as bashful as Jonah. I sometimes wondered about life in our tenant house. Was it altogether silent? When Jonah and Sadie were alone, did they talk?

Before Sadie's first child was born, Mama sent our old cradle up there. It had belonged to Papa's family. Papa and all his brothers and sisters had slept in it, and Grandpa Wister and his brothers before that.

After Jonah's third child was born, he came to see Papa. His brother Frank, in Keyser, had told him there was work for him in a sawmill there, and housekeeping work for Sadie too, and that the pay was good.

"Go ahead, Jonah," Papa said. One October morning, we saw a wagon bumping down our lane with Jonah, Sadie and the baby on the seat. Tucked in at their feet were their two little boys.

Years later, Jonah came back to see us. His small bit of hair had turned completely white, though he was only thirty-seven. With him was one of his sons who had been born in our tenant house. Jonah said this son had just graduated from the twelfth grade, and had been offered a job with the Farmer's and Merchant's Bank. Jonah and Sadie owned their own house.

He told us all this and then, in his old bashful way, turned bright red and stopped talking. Papa saw there was something more he wanted to say.

We all waited. After a moment Jonah went on. "You-all gave me my start," he said. "I mean Mrs. Wister. She done it. She treated me like folks."

MAMA AND THE CHIROPRACTOR

At 26, Mama had the loveliest brown eyes I have ever seen. She had clear pale skin, thick lustrous dark hair and an apparently endless supply of energy. Yet, sometimes the color drained from her face. She pushed herself to her feet, stood a moment stock-still, the way a rabbit does, then—abruptly—she gathered up her skirts and left the room. If I followed her I'd find her door shut. I'd listen. Hearing nothing, I'd tiptoe away, apprehensive.

Sometimes she disappeared into the parlor. Very softly—almost inaudibly—she played "Blessed Assurance" on her old reed organ. Something was wrong.

Around 1904, she made a strange request. She asked me to work the treadle of the sewing machine for her. "The work will go faster if we do it together," she said. Together we pulled the heavy machine away from the window and placed a footstool close to the machine's black iron treadle. Perched on the stool, from the backside of the machine, I started the treadle moving. On the other side of the machine, Mama stitched away, making shirts for my little brothers, dresses for my sisters and me, and nightshirts for Papa.

"Careful now, Nellie," she said, "we're almost at the end of this seam," and I pedaled more slowly. "Now stop," she said, and with a feeling of accomplishment, I stopped. I loved those days when I helped her sew. I loved feeling useful to her.

In 1903, she had her fifth child, my sister Lily. By then Hugh, the younger of my two brothers, was four years old. He asked me, "Why does she go to her room so much, Nellie?"

"I don't know," I answered truthfully.

My other brother complained too. "Dern it, Nellie, what does she do in there?"

"Don't swear, Dayton," I said. I felt uneasy.

It never occurred to any of us that she might not be well. I doubt that it even occurred to Papa, a successful businessman who was away from home much of the time.

Looking back, I now see that Mama was hiding her problem. Wives in those days were expected to have as many babies as the Lord decreed, especially on farms. She didn't want to disappoint Papa.

In 1905, she was expecting her sixth baby. She wore the sort of dress that women in her condition resorted to in those days, a sack-like garment cut full across the front with a drawstring at the waist to control the fullness. For the first time, I noticed that she held one hand inside the opening where the drawstring protruded, as if clutching something there. It was the end of a strip of cloth.

"What's that contraption you're wearing, Carrie?" Mrs. Flood asked one day.

"It's a sling I made to take the weight off my back," Mama said.

Mrs. Flood reported the conversation to Papa, who immediately became concerned. After our latest sister was born, he took Mama to Martinsburg to our Uncle Pent, who was a doctor.

"In the first place, Jack," Uncle Pent said, "haven't any of you looked at her *back*? This condition hasn't come about overnight, you know."

Mama's spinal curvature had started with her first pregnancy, and had worsened with each succeeding child.

Uncle Pent made an appointment with a colleague at Johns Hopkins Hospital in Baltimore. I remember the flurry of preparation for that trip. Mama shut herself in with our local seamstress for days on end. They produced a number of outfits: one of which, I remember, was a pale tobacco-brown linen suit trimmed with wine-colored soutache braid. With it she wore a leghorn hat, the brim decorated with enormous red silk roses.

We children felt at loose ends with Mama gone, yet soon enough she was home again, looking rested. Under her stylish dress she wore a metal brace, constructed of stout bone stays encased in heavy ribbed cotton. It had been prescribed by Uncle Pent's colleague.

It seemed that Mama sometimes ran solely on nervous energy. This became more obvious every day. With terrifying speed, we saw her back grow more distorted. Papa took her to Philadelphia, then to New York. From each journey she came home looking refreshed, bearing presents for each one of us. Each time she wore a heavier and more complicated brace. And as we watched, her small shapely head with its weight of hair appeared to sink between her shoulders. She was twenty-nine years old, still beautiful, still our mother.

At the same time that Mama's body became disfigured, no one could fail to notice the alteration in her expression. Her face showed a kind of withdrawal.

A tenet of Presbyterianism is predestination. "What is to be, shall be," Presbyterians say. Mama, however, raised in that faith, added her own hope to its dour fatalism. Faith in God, she believed, can work wonders.

"They that wait upon the Lord shall renew their strength," I read to her. As I read the passage she had chosen, I stole a glance at her face. Her eyes were closed, her lips moved silently with mine. A serene expression shone on her lovely features. "They shall mount up on wings as eagles, they shall run and not be weary, and they shall walk and not faint." I read, and her lips formed the words with me.

Mrs. Flood, who never went to church, asked Mama one day, "Carrie, you believe, yet look what's happened to you. How do you account for that?"

I realize now that Mama considered her own misfortune scarcely equal to the successions of tragedies in Mrs. Flood's life. Mr. Edgar Flood was alcoholic and died early, Mrs. Flood's stepson was alcoholic, and another stepson committed suicide.

"My *body* may have changed, Emma," Mama said, "but my *life* hasn't."

The Baltimore doctors recommended that she have no more children. However, the births continued unabated until her ninth and final pregnancy in 1917. By that time, she was thirty-nine. I, her oldest child, was twenty-two. Mama had become a hunchback.

A colleague of Papa's, Mr. Woolford, who came every year to hunt in our woods, became alarmed by the change in Mama. He sent her a copy of Mary Baker Eddy's *Science and Health,* and the name of a chiropractor in Harrisonburg, Virginia, across the Shenandoah Mountain from us.

By that time, no one could have done anything to reverse the changes in Mama's spine, but I remember how excited she was by her trips to the chiropractor. The first day after she came home from Harrisonburg, she looked completely refreshed. She threw away her heavy orthopedic brace, saying, "I won't be needing this any more."

Around 1920, I happened to be home, with a mild case of laryngitis. In spite of not feeling well, I drove Mama over the Shenandoah Mountain to her weekly visit with her chiropractor, Dr. Blaikie.

"Dr. Blaikie will give you an adjustment that will cure your laryngitis," she assured me.

He met us on the second floor of a small double frame house in one of Harrisonburg's side streets. A slight, nervous-looking man past middle age, he smelled of Wild Root hair tonic and a popular breath freshener called Sen-Sens. He wore wire-rimmed spectacles with thin, glittering lenses.

"How nice to see you looking so much better, Mrs. Wister!" I understood why she had chosen him: at each appointment, he marveled at how much she had improved.

In Dr. Blaikie's office, Mama changed into a white gown. He assisted her onto a table, then produced an instrument like a pocket watch. Holding it by a chain, He dangled it over her pitifully misshapen body.

He looked at me. "This is a neurocalometer. It shows where your mother's trouble is." He set his gadget aside. Then, with powerful hands for so slight a man, he began to knead Mama's spine.

When he had finished, I put on one of the white gowns and took Mama's place on the table. He dangled his neurocalometer over me. "Look here, Mrs. Wister," he told

Mama, "here's where your daughter's trouble is," and I felt his powerful hands begin to knead my spine.

I sat up. "There's nothing you can do for me," I said in a choked voice. "There's nothing you can do for Mama either." I felt hot all over. I could hardly get the words out. I slid down off the table and headed for the cubicle where I had left my clothes. I couldn't bring myself to look at Mama.

In the Overland, as she and I headed home, she glanced sidewise at me. "You're better, aren't you?" she said. When I didn't answer, she turned away and gazed serenely ahead at the road uncurling before us. "Of course you're better," she said.

Mama told Uncle Pent, "None of you doctors did the slightest thing that really helped me, Pent, but since I've been seeing *Dr. Blaikie*, I've given up *that awful brace* and *those awful stockings.*"

"You have to admit, Jack," Uncle Pent remarked to Papa, "the fellow's smart. We tell her there's nothing we can do. *He* tells her she's better. And she is, in a way. We could learn something from him."

Every day, before anyone else awoke, Mama performed Dr. Blaikie's exercises in the doorway of her bedroom. At night, after everyone else had gone to bed, she performed them again. In the darkened hallway, she pressed her elbows against the narrow doorframe. Without removing them, she walked a few paces forward, then a few paces back. She wore a white sprigged nightgown. Her glorious dark hair hung in a thick rope to her waist. Her face gleamed with such an expression of unfaltering trust that even I found it hard to doubt she was getting better.

BEN ELIOT

Papa said music was important for a girl. By that, he meant playing the reed organ. Everybody we knew owned a reed organ. A worthwhile ambition for a girl was to grow up to play the organ in church. Teachers from the Virginia Conservatory of Music spent their summers in our village. If Mama hadn't married Papa, she'd have studied at the Conservatory.

I was three years old when Mama showed me how to play scales on our reed organ. Grandma Cody had bought it for her when she was my age. By the time I was six, I could play hymns from the *Premier Hymn Book*. At thirteen, I was playing hymns at church.

When I went away to boarding school, Papa and Mama urged me to "keep up my music." At the school, I studied the piano. Until that moment, the only piano I had ever seen or heard was at my Aunt Edith's in Martinsburg. How ugly it looked, I thought. It was too broad and shiny, with no ivory stops to pull out or bellows to pump. And how harsh it sounded– like a tin pan beaten with spoons. In the school's six practice rooms, six girls practiced on six upright pianos. The sounds that seeped through the walls made me think of an elfin orchestra of faint, faraway tin pans. My teacher, Miss Crocker, said the reed organ was out of fashion. She was a small woman with dark hair and eyes, and a slow, soothing, eastern Tennessee way of talking. For her sake I did my best to learn the piano. Soon, to my surprise, I came to appreciate it. Among the selections Miss Crocker taught me were two I especially liked; Dvorzhak's "Humoresque" and a piece called "Snowflakes."

Yet, I missed the homey blended chords of our old reed organ. Nothing relaxed me so much as listening to Miss Crocker play the school's majestic pipe organ.

One Saturday afternoon I had a visitor, a plump young man who said, "I'm Ben Eliot, from Baltimore. I know your cousin Nan Wister in Martinsburg, and since I was passing through, I thought I'd pay my respects."

He wore a loosely fitted grey suit, a soft-collared white shirt, and a narrow grey tie with a four-in-hand knot, held in place by a gold stickpin. He carried a rakish grey cap. I took him on a tour of the school's Confederate Memorial and its two famous, gigantic pine trees. As we approached the school's music building, I said, "Here's where I have my piano lessons."

Something in his manner made me feel he knew this.

"Will you do me the honor of playing for me?" he asked.

In an empty practice room, he sat on the bench beside me while I rattled off my two favorite pieces.

"Why, Miss Wister, I'm impressed!" he exclaimed. "You could play concerts. Your family must be very proud to hear you play."

"We don't have a piano at home," I said. "Besides, I prefer the organ."

Again I had a feeling that he knew this. Nan must have told him. "Oh no!" he exclaimed, "You really must have a piano! Pianos have become so affordable! They are replacing the organ in parlors across America. The reed organ is so limited. One can't do justice to Chopin or Mozart on a reed organ. I hope you'll pardon my saying so."

I thought he was condescending. I said nothing.

The school year ended. I was home one day when doorbell rang. There on the porch stood Mr. Eliot, wearing the same grey suit, gold stickpin and raffish hat. "I was just passing through," he said. "I thought I ought to look in on you folks. I enjoyed so much meeting you at school."

I don't know why I didn't trust Mr. Eliot, but it was late, so I asked him -as I knew Papa would want- if he'd had supper and would he like to stay the night. He accepted, and I showed him to a small bedroom off the upstairs landing. Presently he came downstairs, with his hair carefully slicked, and joined us at supper.

Papa always liked having guests and hearing their stories. He soon found out that Mr. Eliot was a salesman, a drummer, as we called them.

"And what do you sell?" Papa asked.

"Pianos," said our guest.

So that's what this is all about, I thought. He wants to sell us a piano!

"I hope Miss Nellie here will play for us," he said.

I coldly reminded him that we didn't own a piano, only an organ. At this, Mr. Eliot struck his forehead with a small, plump hand. In a half-joking, half troubled tone, as if he were putting a good face on a very bad situation indeed, he turned to Papa. "Mr. Wister, we must do something about this! For Miss Nellie to do well in her music she really must have a piano! The reed organ has fallen quite out of fashion in the cities. The piano is really the instrument of the future. Oh, but I shouldn't be going on like this. I'm a guest here. Please forgive me."

Papa gave Mr. Eliot an appraising look. He smiled at Mama. To my horror, he said, "I've thought of that."

"May I be excused?" I asked, then rose abruptly and left the room.

After supper, Mr. Eliot and Papa sat on the porch. I bitterly regretted that when Mr. Eliot -if that *was* his name- had visited me at school, I hadn't sent him right back to Baltimore.

When I went out to tell Papa goodnight, I found him and Mr. Eliot deep in conversation. It was dusk. I sensed in Mr. Eliot a certain tension, even excitement. In the morning he said, as he pulled out his breakfast chair, "Then shall I have a piano sent on trial, Mr. Wister?"

"I don't want anything sent on trial," Papa said, "I'm placing an order. Show Mrs. Wister here your catalog. Nellie, you'll want to have a look too."

Mr. Eliot bent to rummage inside a small satchel he had carried to the table. With practiced ease, he came up with an illustrated booklet and placed it before Papa.

Papa pushed back his plate to make room. Mama hurried to his side. My sisters Bess and Lily scrambled to get a peek while Elsie and Catherine, six and four, were excited to see the pictures.

"Nellie, which one of these pianos would you like?" Papa asked.

"Whatever you and Mama decide," I answered, annoyed at the whole proceedings.

Papa gave me an odd look as I gathered up some dishes and escaped to the kitchen.

Mama made the ultimate choice: an upright model in a plain mahogany case. The price, delivered, was three hundred and fifty dollars.

"A good choice," Mr. Eliot said as if he were a teacher and Mama his star pupil. "Very, very good. Very."

Until that moment, Mr. Eliot had been quite leisurely. Now, with a snap, he closed his catalogue, pushed back his chair, consulted his gold watch, and held out his hand to Papa. He shook hands with each of my brothers, to their huge satisfaction. He bowed to Mama, my sisters and me.

"I surely will remember you-all," he promised.

I'm sure you will, I thought. Three hundred and fifty times.

As Mr. Eliot left us, I noticed that he had come not in an automobile as I had somehow expected, nor even in a buggy. He drove the kind of old fashioned, boxlike, enclosed vehicle we used to call a "covered wagon," used by peddlers. Mr. Eliot's manner, his gold stickpin and raffish hat had led me to expect something better. Even his gait, now that he was leaving, was like any peddler's—the same quick light step, practically a skip, as he hurried away.

"Where will we put it, Mama?" My brother Dayton asked.

"To the left of the hall door as you come in," Mama answered. "Where the organ is now."

I resented the demotion of the organ, but Mama had made the decision.

The piano had nineteen miles to travel by horse-drawn wagon, from the nearest train depot to our house. Baxter and Sam Flood ran a hauling freight business, using a road wagon and four enormous dray horses.

"You'll need both teams for that piano," Papa told them.

One evening they appeared in our lot. Up on the seat beside them was Burz Clayton, a big man capable of wrestling a piano, or anything else, off a road wagon. From the house, all we could see of the piano was its shape under a big tarpaulin. Peeking at the wooden piano crate under the tarp, my little sister Catherine said, "There's our new playhouse!"

The men removed the front of the box. Heavy timbers lay ready to slide the piano up onto the porch. With grunts and heaves, they tilted the massive instrument out of the wagon, and uncrated it. They rolled it slowly on smooth logs across the yard, slid it up the porch steps on the timbers, then, on it's own wheels, across the porch and into the parlor. Unceremoniously, my old companion, the organ, was shoved aside. On the count of three, the men rolled the piano into place.

Breathing heavily and wiping their faces, the men admired the piano. Everyone admired it. I was the only person present who had ever played a piano, or even seen one.

Mama sensed my reluctance to take the lead. She sat down on the shiny new bench and played "When the Roll is Called Up Yonder." Her small feet moved habitually, as if pumping the organ's bellows. The ice broken, I joined her and clattered through "Snowflakes" and "Humoresque."

"It has a very good tone," I said.

"It will need to be tuned," was Mama's contribution.

Each of my sisters got a turn to run her fingers over the keys. Our hired girls, with freshly washed hands, had a try.

"I like the organ better," said Ola. We all fell silent.

Like everything new, our piano was a subject of great curiosity among our neighbors. Maud Flood arrived to look it over and, to my surprise, play a few chords. Her mother gave it a try, and so did Mrs. Righter, though her old fingers were stiff. The Neff children and the

Morgans came. Children arrived whom we barely knew. Some we had never even seen because they lived up above the poor farm, across the river, or on Duncan's Creek. Everyone was made to wash his hands, and everyone got a chance.

One Saturday afternoon, when I thought I was alone in the house, I heard someone playing the piano downstairs. No tunes, just discordant notes, and very softly. I hurried downstairs to investigate. There sat Lettie Morgan.

Lettie was six years old. She had her father's mischievous black eyes. When we installed our bathroom, she was the first to try the tub—naked and uninvited.

Looking around from the piano bench, Lettie grinned at me. "I washed my hands," she said.

I sat down, and together we played scales. For days, until she tired of it, Lettie came to our house. She stopped by the outdoor sink to wash her hands, then went straight to the parlor, shut herself in, and ran through scales.

On Sundays at bedtime, I accompanied our evening hymns on the piano, although, to our ears, it had the wrong sound. Soon, to everyone's relief, Mama requested we move back to the faithful organ where, with a patient, forgiving air, it waited on the other side of the doorway. In its soft, familiar tones, I played "Blest Be the Tie that Binds", "Now the Day Is Over", and Papa's favorite, "The Church in the Wildwood." These old hymns sounded right again.

One day Papa ran into his old friend, Mr. Eddie Sanderson, in Minerva. Mr. Eddie said, "That young friend of yours from Baltimore was here, Jack.

"What young friend from Baltimore?" Papa asked.

"Sells pianos," Mr. Eddie said. "I bought one for Sylvia, same model you bought for Nellie. Ed Teter bought one for

Alice. Ben Hoyt bought one for Helen, and Joe Huddleston bought one for his Minnie. She ain't but a little thing yet, but he wants her to get the jump on some of the other girls around here."

"Oh, him." Papa said. "Fine fellow. Good pianos too."

The following summer, Mr. Eliot came back to Chinkapin Creek. Grandpa Cody ordered a player piano for my Aunt Nan, who, he admitted, was too unfocused to learn a regular instrument. Uncle Virgil ordered a standard upright, and so did Neffs. For his sales in Chinkapin Creek, Mr. Eliot got a promotion.

The followed summer he stopped by our house. "I was just passing through, and thought I'd look in on you folks," he said.

"You want to sell us another piano?" I asked him. I could barely bring myself to look him in the face.

All he wanted was supper and a bed for the night. He sat on the porch with Papa for only the time that seemed polite. In the morning, he hurried away.

Pianos never caught on in our community, but I learned something about smooth talking salesmen. Mr. Eliot sold dozens of pianos in our county, but few of them were ever played. On Sunday evenings, the rich harmonies of reed organs echoed through the darkening hills.

CPSIA information can be obtained at www.ICGtesting.com
Printed in the USA
LVOW081449280513

335796LV00001B/42/P